T0162654

LAST BATTLE
for
MANIA

THE FIGHT BEFORE THE WAR ON EARTH

TIBERIU GANEA

Order this book online at www.trafford.com
or email orders@trafford.com

Most Trafford titles are also available at major online book retailers.

Printed in the United States of America.

ISBN: 978-1-4669-6747-2 (sc)
ISBN: 978-1-4669-6749-6 (hc)
ISBN: 978-1-4669-6748-9 (e)

Library of Congress Control Number: 2012922545

Trafford rev. 11/27/2012

 www.trafford.com

North America & international
toll-free: 1 888 232 4444 (USA & Canada)
phone: 250 383 6864 ♦ fax: 812 355 4082

LAST BATTLE *for* MANIA

When something ends, almost in the same moment, something starts; for in every end you can find a new beginning. Let's take life, for example. When somebody's life ends, another one starts. Somebody may be born exactly in the same moment. Also, maybe the reciprocity is true.

Everything in this story had happened two millennia ago. Everyone knows that when our savior Jesus came on Earth, a star was shining on the sky, the one that guided the three lords in their journey, when they were searching the place where Jesus was born.

Everyone from those days had seen a star on the sky—a star everyone could see from all places of world. It was the most shining star that anyone could ever see. This star tells everyone that, here on Earth, a new king was born, an emperor whose powers are beyond anyone's expectations.

But all this can be read in the Bible. This story is not about us but about another planet and another people. It's about a faraway planet, a planet that was situated close of that shining star.

While for us it was a new beginning, maybe for others it was their end. Those kinds of thoughts make you think when our end will come. When will the apocalypse of our planet be? Next year, over a month, tomorrow, today—now? Only the one who wrote all about the apocalypse in the Bible knows how hard it will be when those days will come on our planet. Only he and God know when those days will come, and every people will suffer on those days. Everyone—Americans, Europeans, Asians—there will be no compromise because in the front of God everyone is equal until the last days; the apocalypse will be here on Earth. The words of the Bible sounds like this: "Those that have ears hear what tells the Holy Spirit to the Churches: Only to those that wins I will give him to eat from the sky's food, and I'll give him a white rock; and on that rock is been writing a new name, which name, only the one who gets it, will know it."

The Bible also said, "Only to those who win, they will be dressed with white clothes. I won't delete his name from the Life Book, and I will tell his name to My Father and his angels."

But how many people understand the meaning of these words? How many people listen to these words, and how many of them will fight against evil by doing only good things? Making good things is only the beginning of the fight. From the words of the Bible, you can understand that a battle is near us—a battle that we must win. Perhaps another people had fought in this battle. Maybe some of them won this battle, and some of them lost it.

The Bible says that if you obey the words of God, then you shouldn't be afraid of this war. But a lot of people don't care what these words say. A lot of them don't care about God's will. And because of them, we all will suffer. We will suffer anyway. We will suffer if we chose the way of God. We will suffer if we chose the evil way. But we all know that if we chose God, we suffer a while, but after the apocalypse and after the Lord of the Dark Satan will be defeated, all this suffering will be transformed to rejoicing.

Those that took God's parts will be in heaven, the others will be in hell. Where is your destination? You can tell it yet from your life on Earth. The good things that you did in your life will decide which one is your destination. Good things means heaven; bad things means hell.

If you are a pious man, you will be in heaven. If you are bad, then only the gates of hell will be opened for you. But maybe this is not all true. Perhaps only after one last war, the war the Bible says, will you know your destination.

In this war, which the Bible speaks about, the people from Earth will fight. All of us will fight in it. And maybe other civilizations from this universe will fight in this war because probably there are other civilizations on other faraway planets. And surely we have the same God, and surely we are equal in front of him. He loves us the same because all of us are his sons. We must pass through all the difficulties that evil has sent to us.

We don't know when the end will come. Perhaps other civilizations from other planets also don't know. Perhaps some of them have known. Doubtless is that the people from one planet called Mania knows that their end is close enough, but they didn't know exactly that moment. So most of them were taken by surprise. Perhaps we also will be taken by surprise when our time will come!

Two millennia ago, a planet called Mania, situated near the star that was shining when Jesus was born, was affected by all these troubles—troubles the Bible speaks about. This planet is almost the size of Earth. The people that had lived there two millennia ago were also almost same as us, only that they were a little bit smaller. Like us, some of them chose the way of God; others chose the evil's way. The ones that chose the evil didn't obey the prophets sent by God to help them reach the right way. Just like on Earth. Some of them were listening to the Father, the Creator of the universe, the One that separated the night from the day, and last but not the least the One that created them. "The Lord of the light" is the name they used to speak about the Creator. They also named him the Creator, the Father, the Wiser, and all other names that overbless God. These names we people of Earth use when we speak about God.

But the majority were ruled by Voron, the serpent, which we all know as Satan. At the beginning, when God offered them all that they wanted, Satan, named by the people from Mania as Voron, convinced Rasan—the mother of the human beings of Mania, mother of the "manits," the people that lived on Mania—to choose the possibility of knowing the bad things also. The same mistake Eve, our mother, chose to make when the snake offered her "the apple." Who knows how Voron managed to lie and trick Rasan and her husband, Bornir? They did the same mistake like Adam and Eve.

At the beginning of Mania's creation, Rasan and Bornir made a big mistake, one that maybe any human being could make. They chose to know not only the right but also the evil.

And Voron the serpent was very happy then. He wanted hate and war to rule on Mania and on all other planets.

He sent some of his lying prophets to speak about the domination of the strong people against the weak. In some occasions, he went himself on Mania as a great prophet and tried to trick the manits over the possibility of taking from the others whatever is missing from their home. He spoke about hate, death, destruction, and the absence of the Creator.

"If the Creator is inside of you, if He is with you, then why didn't he give you what you need? Why does he let you to die because of disease? Why does he let animals kill your brother, wife, or friend? Does he listen to you when you need His help?"

He also said some words about how they had managed to discover all the inventions that they used in their lives. The animals they managed to domesticate were a result of their intelligence, and they did these without their "Lord's" help.

"Did your Lord came to you and say to you, you can domesticate this animal or that creature? He didn't. So all these happened only thank to you," Voron said to the manits.

Even the manits weren't technologically advanced like us; they thought that they were very artful. They thought no other planet was as advanced as they are. Their technology was almost the same as the one our ancestors had known two millennia ago. They knew how to make and use weapons. They also knew about machines like catapults or like the one that threw spears over a long distance. They were almost as advanced as the Roman Empire people. Or maybe the Romans were the as advanced as the manits were.

So using his wiliness, Voron tried to make the manits blaspheme God, forcing them not to believe in Him:

"There is no Creator. Does anyone tell you how to do that, how to work on that? No. You discover it because you are the most intelligent creature on this planet, because you need to make your day-by-day life easy!"

Some of them eventually stopped believing in the Creator. Others didn't care about the Creator because they were occupied with daily's problems. And others—who knows? Perhaps they will never believe that in this universe is someone that creates everything we manage to see.

Because of all this, Lord of the Light, the God that created the universe and all the planets, sent all kinds of curses on Mania. Like the Bible says, "And the first angel blow in his trumpet. And it came hail and fire mixed with blood, which were threw on Mania; and the third part of Mania has been burned and the third part of trees has been burned and all the green grass has been burned."

The words of the Lord of the Light, once said by Him through the prophet's mouth, took place, and all these curses hit Mania—and probably soon will hit Earth.

Then "the second angel blows in his trumpet. And something as a big mountain of fire has been thrown into the sea; and the third part of the sea became blood. And the third part of the creatures that lived into the sea had died . . . . And the third angel blows in his trumpet. And a big star was fallen from the sky, which was flamed up like a torch; it has been fallen over the third part of the rivers and over the waters. And the name of the star is Pelin. And the third part of the waters had become pelin and a lot of people died because of the waters, because the waters became bitter."

All these curses struck the planet called Mania, and lots of the people that lived before those days on this planet were dead. Most of the rivers and lakes disappeared from the surface because of the heat. Almost all the water that this planet still had was under the surface. All the great strongholds placed everywhere now were missing. Only few of those strongholds spared by the Lord of Light still showed their walls on the planet's surface.

Banits is the name of the people that lived in one stronghold called Megros, on one side of the river with the same name. After the Lord of the Light struck Mania with a lot of curses, the majority of the places from this planet were erased from the surface. Fire and diseases destroyed everything. Only a few of them were protected from those curses by the mercy of the Creator.

The few zones that still had water, stoked in lakes, were supplied by underground waters. The only outside huge river was Megros. In the ancestor's language, Megros means "the tears of God." They called this river Megros because the surface of their planet at one time was filled with water; now it is a desert because only a few places have water on the surface. One of these is Megros, the place where God let his tears form a river. This is the belief of banit's ancestors and his too.

Other rivers were much smaller, though more water was hiding under the surface of the planet.

At the beginning, before Megros's appearance on banit's maps, there were some greater cities. But there were two great cities the chronics spoke about.

Sodoria was one of them. Sodoria, in the ancestor's language, means "the town where the Lord never enters" because all the people from this town were living in salacity. People killed their brothers, stole from each other, and people killed each other for no reason. There were fornication, blasphemy against the Lord of Light, and stealing for no reason.

A second city was on the other side of Megros, the other bank of the river. It was Martos. The people from Martos were best soldiers and builders. "Martos's fortress had had some high towers; from them you could see all the mountains from Mania," said the old people to the young banits. "Their walls were also huge. Not even five banits holding by their hands and then disperse can be as thick as the wall."

There were many such stories about the two areas. The banit's ancestress said old stories about Sodoria and Martos.

Only those who believed in the Creator from Sodoria and Martos were alive these days. They had built new fortresses, and one of them was the town called Megros. The most beautiful gardens were in this city. The banits, people from Megros, were peaceful. They had weapons but only to protect themselves. They didn't have assault weapons. The river with the same name was also one of the rivers that hadn't dried up—perhaps the only one river. The banits might not have known about other people, others towns, or other rivers. Ever since those curses started to strike Mania for almost one thousand years, the banits didn't have the courage to walk on long distances. They lived near their town. They had the gardens and hunted around Megros fields. Sometimes they entered into the woods to hunt. The woods were a one mile away from the town. The trees that composed the woods, called imensialiss, were higher than anyone can imagine. They were the highest trees from Mania., towering more than three hundred meters. The diameter of these trees was more than fifteen meters. The treetop began at fifteen meters from the ground, so almost any creature can walk through these woods without any problem, even the big ones. Because the woods hid many dangers, the banits tried to avoid hunting in the woods. Almost every time they entered in the woods, some of the persons from the group were killed by huge animals.

Even at this time, the last hunt before everything changed on Mania. This time only one person of the group survived: Aarnos.

Never Aarnos had run so quickly. In a few "period," he ran almost two miles. When he just came out from the woods, he became calmer. In the woods he can be attacked any time; but if he can be out, he would have a chance. If the creatures that killed the entire group were behind him, maybe the sentinels that were staying on the walls will see him and they will come to help him.

"Are those creatures following me?" he kept asking himself. But he did not have the courage to look back. He didn't want to see the death that was taking him.

"Why did we enter into the woods?" was another question that bothered him. "Why?"

Everyone knew that those woods were more dangerous than anything else. Almost every night, when he and the others looked at the woods from the high walls, they could see big animals— huge creatures. Many of them lived in the woods, and sometimes some of them got out for a few moments. Most of them were taller, almost two or three times than the banits. But others had only their head at that size.

Aarnos was so close to his town. Now he can see that something was happening at the gate, on the walls. Some people from the town got out, including some soldiers.

"Those creatures are following me! Lord, please help me!" said Aarnos, and he started to run more quickly. He ran and ran, until finally he was at the gate.

Maybe the Lord listened to his prayers. Behind him was no creature. The sentinel saw him alone, and because he didn't know why he was alone, he sounded the bell. The soldiers got out through the gate after the sentinel gave the signal, prepared to fight if it's necessary.

Aarnos was inside the stronghold now, and he was so tired. He had no wounds, but he looked like he was more dead than alive. Some persons approached him. They were from the high council of this town. But Aarnos couldn't speak to anyone maybe because he was tired or he was too much frightened. His only word was "Efreu."

It was a lovely day. There was no heat, no cold—like it should be. Efreu—a prophet sent by the Most High, an old man—was sitting on a chair in front of his hut. He was the Creator's voice. Through his voice and words, the Lord managed to guide the men from Megros toward the right way.

While his mind was elsewhere, a young man approached. He was Emos, the son of Dethretus. The residents of Megros believed that Emos was a descendant of the nation destroyed by the Creator. They felt that there was a problem of time before the Creator will destroy him like he did with his ancestors. Even if the banits were also the descendants of the people from Sodoria, they say that they were the descendants of those who listened and believed in the Lord of Light. Emos's family was one of the most terrifying families in Sodoria; the great-grandfather of his grandfather was merciless.

"It's such a beautiful day," said Emos to Efreu. The young man watched the prophet for a while in his meditation. At first he thought he should leave and not disturb him, but then, because a problem was bothering him too much, he took his courage and tried to speak with him.

Awakened from his deep thoughts, Efreu replied, "I know why you came, dear boy."

Embarrassed because Efreu knew everything about him, Emos let down his look. He was the kind of man that didn't let anyone to read his mind. His warrior's blood that flowed in his veins made him a little sharp. Although he was a very skilled fighter and handled a sword better than anyone, he was a gentle and calm man.

"How is Adela?"

"I saw her again . . . yesterday. And her father saw us at the Blue Garden."

The banits called that place the Blue Garden because of the great fountains that were all over the place. The banits built some kind of aqueducts to help the vegetation from the garden to become a luxurious one. The Blue Garden was the most beautiful gardens in Megros.

After a few moments the young man continued, "And he asked me again to leave his daughter alone . . . forever . . . to understand once and for all that all I do is destroying her life."

"So you came to me because you want me to speak with her father and tell him that you are a good man and that you will be a great husband for her."

Emos said nothing. But he looked down again.

"Don't worry. I will speak with him," said Efreu, and he returned to his thoughts.

He sat and thought about something—something that obviously bothered him. His eyes seemed to express pain, fear, and helplessness.

Efreu was a little bit scared. But he tried not to show that. Last night he had a dream, a premonition God sent to him. Even Efreu didn't understand the meaning of that dream because Aarnos had appeared in that dream. Efreu had dreamed one last night that in one day he woke up and everything was so real for him. His home, his bed, all his furniture—everything looked so real. But even if he knew that it was morning, the sun didn't rise.

"What could have happened," he asked.

He went to one of his neighbors' door, and he knocked. No answer. Everything was so silent. The animals were awaked. But none of his people were outside.

He knocked again—nothing.

"Where is everyone? They should be at work. The sheep are out; even the roster is outside. It's clear that it is morning now," he thought. "But none is outside; none is inside. What could have happened to them?"

Efreu began to run in his dream as fast as he can at his age. He began to run from door to door and knocked at every door he reached. But he got no answer. He continued to run and run. Finally he saw someone near one of the town's gates: the one from the east. Now that he saw someone, he could breathe more easily because he didn't have to run anymore. He was more relieved because he can find out what had happened.

He approached that person, and he saw that was Aarnos, one of the many young ones that often had come to Efreu to listen his stories about God, stories from their Holy Book. Efreu often had tried to make his people to understand what the Holy Book said. And he knew this better than anyone because he was the man of God. The man whom God spoke to whenever He wanted to say something to the banits.

"Where is everyone?" Efreu asked the boy.

The same answer: nothing.

"Aarnos? Are you fine, Aarnos?"

But Aarnos didn't answer. He kept looking to the east. But why? Everyone knew that centuries ago, God had vanished everything that was on that zone. They used to be two great cities, but now there was only dust, ruins, and ashes.

"Aarnos, why don't you answer me? It's not nice to let an old man speak alone." And he smiled, and he touched the boy on the shoulder with his left hand because in his right hand he was keeping his stick. When he touched him, he was shocked. The boy was cold as ice, so cold that Efreu awoke from his dream.

Efreu woke up from his dream, relieved. He got off his bed. He put some water in an antique-like glass, the kind our ancestors used in their lifetime. But when he wanted to grab the object with water in it, the water turned into ice. This event terrified the old man. "First that dream and now this event. The Creator wants to tell me something," thought Efreu. It's been a long time since he received the last divination. The last one had been when God told him that there will be five years of drought. And so it was.

"But what does He want to tell me right now? And why didn't he send me a messenger?" thought Efreu this morning. "The drought came after two plentiful years. Let's hope that if it is something bad, it will come after many years."

All those bad thoughts bothered him while he was inside his dark house. But when he came out and he saw that it was such a nice weather outside, he became calmer. There was not a cloud or a breath of wind. All was nice and calm outside, so Efreu the Wise couldn't be anything else than happy. He sat down on a bench right in front of his house. He looked at the people running away to resolve their problems.

Some of the neighbors were carrying goods, others arranging their yards. All of them were doing something.

Two of his neighbors were speaking about Aarnos and others of his age. One of them said to the other that those young men were gone for hunting for an entire week.

When he heard that Aarnos will be gone for over one week, Efreu smiled. He thought that whatever the premonition was, everything will happen after a long time.

But as anyone knows, not everything happens like one wants. So it was with Efreu—for the banits.

"Great Efreu! Great Efreu!" yelled someone.

The young man who was running so quickly and yelling so strong was Aarnos

"God, please protect us," said the wise man, terrified.

And he should be.

"Wise Efreu, help us!" yelled Aarnos again.

"Calm down," said the wise man. "Tell me what happened."

The young man said everything so fast. Everything was so unbelievable that Efreu didn't understand anything. "Tell me again everything you said and more calmly so I can understand what you're saying."

Aarnos breathed intensely and began to say his story more slowly, "We were close to Megros. When we set up our camp to rest for tomorrow's hunt, some strange animals attacked us. It was dark. But I could see that those animals were the biggest animals I have ever seen. And all of them were unfamiliar for all of us, even bigger than our horses."

The banits weren't familiar with big animals. They heard the stories about them, but except one or two of the oldest, nobody had seen any big animal.

"Where are your brothers?" asked Efreu.

"I lost them. I hope that I will find them here. But I see that none of them is here."

Aarnos's voice trembled. You can see on his face that he was suffering for his lost friends.

Tears began to flow on his face. The boy was frightened. Efreu knew that it will be worse than now. But he can't tell Aarnos or anyone of his people what he was thinking at that moment, not until he has spoken with The guardian. So even if he knew that some of Aarnos's brothers and friends wouldn't be back—maybe none of them—he said to Aarnos, "Don't worry too much. You'll see, they will be here by midnight."

"Maybe I should stay and help them. Maybe I should go back for them. We should go back for them."

"You can't do anything for them. None of us can. Those creatures are more dangerous than you think."

"But I want to help my brothers. I want to kill many of those creatures . . . to fight with them."

Into the boy's body flowed the blood of a hunter, so he was very enthusiastic when he thought about killing so many dangerous creatures. Who knows when he will have this chance again?

Efreu answered to the young man, "Aarnos, you can't do any harm to them."

"Efreu, but I am—"

"Young man!" yelled the wise. "Don't you understand what I said? We can't kill those beasts. Our weapons do not harm them!"

Aarnos was shocked but not because of what Efreu said but because of how he said all those words. He had never seen Efreu so angry. Nobody had, because no matter what the situation was, Efreu always was very calm. Now something was different— more different—and that frightened Aarnos more than those creatures.

Some people who were near Efreu and Aarnos heard parts of their conversation. All of them stopped working, especially when they had heard Efreu yelling at Aarnos. Even those who were a little bit far from them came to see what was happening.

One banit came and asked Aarnos something. He didn't have the courage to ask Efreu.

"What's happening, Aarnos? I saw you running like the ends are coming."

But the one who answered to the man was Efreu, not Aarnos.

"Maybe the end is coming, or at least it's near."

All those who got around Efreu and Aarnos were very surprised and frightened because of those words. Everything Efreu said in his life was very serious. He never had joked about anything. So all of them, all the banits, should be frightened.

When he saw the crowd so scared, Efreu tried to rise up their morale, "For every end, there is a beginning. The end is also the one who takes us to the eternal life. So we shouldn't be scared if we believe in God.

"And everything is true. The end of our mortal life means the beginning of a new and better life if we believe in the Creator of the universe. But we should know that the hardest period for mortals is the period between these two worlds. This is the hardest, and Efreu knows that."

No one said anything for a short while. Everyone was still frightened. Efreu's words didn't help at all. So the wise broke the silence. "Tell the elders that I have to speak with them," said Efreu to the man that asked Billy about what happened to him.

The man disappeared immediately into the crowd, and everyone who heard that the council of the elders was meeting went to tell to rest of banits about that. This meeting meant that something important was happening. The elder and Efreu rarely got together, only when they had something really important to speak.

"As you know, something terrible happened. Our sons, our cousins, went to hunt some animals for our community. But only one of them returned until now. The others—" Efreu had made a short break, and he continued. "The others didn't return, and we have less hope that they will."

Efreu told these words in front of the elders: the council of the wisest. But the meeting was kept outside, in Norus's yard. It was a large place, so everyone can listen to what was spoken about. From old banits to adults and children—all of them gathered in Norus's yard. Norus was looking almost the same age as Efreu. Maybe they had the same age. But the fact was that if everybody knew that Norus was almost sixty years old; nobody knew exactly how old Efreu was.

"They have the same age," everyone was saying.

When it was Norus's birthday, friends would bring presents for Efreu too. And Efreu accepted them without saying anything. He just thanked them for the presents.

But this was not very important. Not now. What we should know is that all the most important banits were gathering in Norus's yard. And a few hundreds of children, adults, and other old men were there too.

There was a lot of noise; everyone was talking nearby.

Efreu rose his right hand. In a few moments everybody stopped speaking, so Efreu could tell them what he wanted to discuss. "All of us know the words of our Creator, words that we can find in the

Book of Knowledge. And any of us had heard from our ancestors about those signs."

Efreu paused in between his sentences. He looked at the audience. Almost everyone was scared. He continued, "About fire which long time ago had fallen from the sky . . . about those pieces of stars . . . And lots of those who once lived in peace on this planet are dead. From what we know, we are the only survivors."

A lot of noise came from all around. The banits began to speak about the disaster that fell upon them. Efreu didn't say anything about it, but all of them knew that the end was closer than they thought. So what Efreu thought will be a surprise for them was not.

Now Efreu can speak to his people about what was the most important. "We should know what the Book of Knowledge, the Holy Book, said. For those who don't know, listen carefully now." And he began to read:

> The fifth Angel blow in his trumpet. And I saw one star which fell from the sky. He received the key of the Deep Fountain and he opened it. From the fountain the smoke raised up, lots of smokes just like the smoke of a huge clamp. And the sun and the sky became dark because of the smoke.
>
> From the sky came out some locusts . . . . And those locusts received strength, like the strength of shrews. They must harm no grass, no greens, and no tree . . . only those people who hadn't on their head God's seal.
>
> Those locusts looked like some kind of war horses. On their head they had some kind of gold crowns. Their faces were like banits' faces.
>
> They had their hair like woman's hair and fangs like the beasts have. They had iron breastplates and the sound of their wings was like the sound of lots of chariots dragged by many horses which throw themselves in battle.

They had tails with awns. And in their tails were the strength.
Their leader was the Emperor of the Deep, which name's was Abadon.

After he read this paragraph from the Book of Knowledge, Efreu looked around. Everyone was terrified. They knew what kind of creatures attacked Billy and the others: creatures like those from the Book of Knowledge.

From the crowd came Rasus, one of the elders. He came near Efreu and said while he looked at the crowd, "We all know that you are our adviser, the wisest, but we have to fight against these creatures. I spoke with Billy, and he told me that you said to him that our weapons won't harm those creatures."

"Those were my words."

"But we must destroy those beasts. Our lands must be protected. If we don't attack them, our lands will be infested by them. And soon they will be in our castle killing our children and wives."

"Those creatures, which this young saw, can't be killed."

"We must try. We must save our lands and homes."

"You should know something else. Maybe many of you knew it already. Something more terrible, more destructive will come upon us. Let me read it to you." Efreu opened again the Book of Knowledge, and he began to read:

The first catastrophe has passed. The sixth Angel blow into his trumpet. And I heard a voice saying to the sixth angel who had the trumpet: "Release the four angels." . . . And the four angels, who were waiting for that hour, day, month and year were released, to kill the third part of people.

And this is how it has been shown to me in my vision the horses and riders: they had breastplates looking like fire and sulfur.

The horse's heads were like the heads of beasts,
and from their mouth they throw fire, smoke and
sulfur. And their tails were like snakes with heads,
and with them they harmed.

"Then tell us what we must do with these horses and riders.
How will we manage to attack and destroy them?" spoke Rasus
again.

"I do not know how we could destroy them, Rasus."

Hearing these words made the crowd extremely quiet.

Everyone was shocked. The banits never heard such an answer
from Efreu. He never replied saying that he doesn't know how to
resolve something. It was so quiet. You can even hear the voices
in the back . . . people saying to those from outside, to those who
couldn't find a place in Norus's yard because it was full, what
happen . . .

Efreu broke the silence:

"If we try to destroy these creatures, we won't succeed. The
only thing we can do is to defend and try to resist them."

"Then we shall defend ourselves. Let's prepare what we need
to defend ourselves—immediately."

These words were said by Sindur, a very good soldier.

"I'm glad that you are so eager to defend your people, Sindur,"
said Efreu. He put his left arm on Sindur's shoulder and smiled at
him. Then he continued to speak while he looked at the crowd,
"But those whom you will fight are much too strong to be defeated
by you. And it is not possible to defend the castle Megros. We
should go to Amnus, known as the Citadel of Our Lord. You must
take with you only food and weapons—all the weapons you have—
because we will need them."

Then Efreu rose up and moved toward the door of the house
of Norus. But just when he wanted to go outside, he heard a voice.
Norus spoke, "Wise Efreu, but here is our life. We cannot leave
these lands so easy. Here is our wealth; here is everything we
collect in our life."

Many of those who took part at that meeting had the same thoughts as Norus. They didn't want to leave their homes. Efreu saw that, so he told to everyone with a strong voice, "We agree with Norus. Just wait until tomorrow. I'll try to speak with Gabriel."

"We will meet tomorrow morning here. And after that, we'll see what God prepares for us; everyone will decide what he is going to do," Norus said.

Efreu left Norus's yard. The crowd did the same. Everyone went to his house.

Efreu entered inside his house. There he had a small room, daggered into a mountain. That room was a big cave with a door that can be opened or closed just by the inside. When he was outside the room, the door was slightly open, but when he was inside the room, he struck the door with a strong bolt.

Once again he came inside and looked at the door. He sat down on a rug and started to pray strongly.

"Please, Lord, send your servant Gabriel so he can advise me on what to do next because, as you know, my Lord, it is very difficult to convince many of the banits to come to the fortress that You gave us for such events. Please don't leave us, God. You, the Creator of heavens and universes and have given us our life, please send Your servant Gabriel to help us."

Just after he said all these words, a little light came up inside the dark room. And Efreu knew that it was the divine presence no one can enter inside the room. Even a speck of light can't, only a divine being.

"Or something evil," said Efreu with a low voice.

The wise looked with fear at the appearance. It was not Gabriel. Gabriel had a long hair, slightly wavy and blonde. He looked like a banit. He was dressed every time with a white silk shirt, embroidered with gold. The one that came looked like an angel, but he had black hair—same long and slightly wavy hair but black—and he was wearing over that shirt embroidered with gold a gold armor. On the armor were some long-forgotten engraved words, a sacred language not heard for thousands of years. This language was once used by the banits' ancestors, when sin was missing entirely from the life of those who were living on Mania. Once sin appeared on this planet, there appeared the difference between the languages spoken by people from Megros, Sodomits, and Gomorits. In time, this language was definitely lost. Just a few words were known by the priests and older prophets. Even Efreu barely spoke this language. Not much was known. When Gabriel came to him, they usually spoke in their familiar language: the banit.

And when he showed himself to Efreu, Gabriel was as tall as a banit. This angel was more than five times taller than a banit, and his face is covered with a gold mask. His sword and his shield could easily cut a house in two pieces or smashed it. The angel could scare anybody.

The angel saw the old man was terrified, so he spoke with a mild voice, "Do not be afraid, Efreu. The Lord of Light sent me to talk to you. I'm Michael, another captain of the Lord's army. The seraphim's captain."

When he heard that the angel was the servant of His Lord, Efreu raised his eyes; he looked at the angel and breathed more easily. He always wanted to see an angel in his splendor because he knew that the Creator's servants took the form of a banit so they didn't want to scare them. He also knew that if he will have this chance, which means that something very bad is going to happen.

Michael continued to speak, "The Lord told me to prepare you for what might come. This battle you have to wear, it also have to be worn by other people from other planets."

Efreu didn't say anything. He was much too scared to ask anything. So many questions flew through his mind, but he couldn't ask any.

Michael continued to speak, answering to some of the old man's questions, "Some of them have been won. More of them have been lost. Those who have won are now at the Lord's bosom. They have become the army of heaven."

"What about the others?"

"The others are the army of darkness, army of the dark Lord, Voron. They outnumber us and come from all kinds. If Voron would send his army, even with our army, I don't think that you'll win. But Voron can send on Mania only those armies mentioned in the Holy Book, the army from the planet where the war took place. In this case, it's about your planet Mnia and the creatures and the people from it. This is what the Lord commanded Voron, the great evil enemy."

"What do you mean you will not help us in this fight?"

"We cannot interfere in this fight unless Voron, the Lord of Darkness, will intervene too much. And he often did so. And when he did so, the Creator sent us. Hardly had we defeated Voron. We lost many friends, and their souls were taken by Voron."

Efreu was destroyed. If the Holy Army of angels hardly managed to defeat Voron's army, then the people from Megros had already lost.

"We won't succeed," said Efreu to Michael. "It's impossible for us to destroy the army of Voron."

"You shouldn't try to destroy it. Even if you meet a small part of this army, then you'll be destroyed in this moment," Michael replied.

"And those who do not want to come with us?"

"They have the right to choose. Just like any of you."

Efreu didn't say anything.

"For now you should start to go to Amnus fortress, a choice that you already did. A good choice, on measure of your wisdom, Efreu. Only there will you be able to defend your people. In any other place, you will lose forever. Leave these lands just right away. In the dawn of day, it would be better. Let the light guide you, and this will help you in your fight against the evil creatures.

"What kind of creatures? How can we fight against them? Help us to defend ourselves, Michael."

"You will find those beasts that your brothers saw and other kinds of beasts, which probably even I do not know anything about them. Just Voron, their master, and our Lord, the Omniscient, only they know. But I tell you: the only thing you can do if you meet them is to run."

On Efreu's face you can see more and more fear.

So Michael tried to help him, "But I give you this bottle with water from wells of Amnus fortress. Holy water. If your arms are touched by the holy water, then you may have a chance to kill such a creature. But the best is to run from their way until you'll be into our Lord's fortress, Amnus. But remember: the power of our Lord will be by your side but only inside the Amnus walls. Remember this."

And Michael prepared to leave.

"Wait a minute please," called Efreu for Michael. "I still have some questions that are bothering me."

"All you need to know you already know. We'll meet again at the fortress of our Lord. There we will continue our discussion."

And Michael disappeared.

Efreu was once again left in that perfect darkness. He stayed alone and thought about the terrible fate banits had to follow. Only the Creator knew what was going to happen. Will they be okay? It was impossible that everything will be fine. But will it be bad or very bad?

Once again the council of the elders met. Efreu was speaking in front of the crowd but he was especially speaking to the elders. They sat down on some chairs disposed in a semi-circle. Here in Norus's yard, there were a lot of chairs and tables for the crowd. But still they were not enough. More than three quarters were still standing up.

"I spoke with our Lord's sender," began Efreu. "He said that the only thing we can do is to go to Amnus. There we'll meet him again. He will tell us what to do next."

"Does Gabriel say that we can't kill those creatures?"

"I didn't meet Gabriel. I meet Michael, another angel."

"Michael?" asked some of the elders in one voice. "Have you ever seen him? Are you sure that he is the Creator's angel too?"

"Yes, I'm sure."

"Well, I am not," said Sindur. "From what we all read, the Lord of Light said that if you are trying to harm someone with your sword, by sword you'll die. So those creatures that attacked us with their 'swords,' those beasts will die by sword. Our swords!" yelled Sindur.

These words made that tensed crowd to explode. More than half of them began to yell, "Let's fight with them! Let's kill them!"

"Do not fight for what we have collected in our lives!"

But the people didn't listen what Efreu still had to say.

"Let's kill them!"

"Do not fight for the castle, the houses, and places . . . for objects."

There was so much noise. From what one can hear and see, more than a half of the banits wanted to stay and fight in Megros.

Efreu thought to himself that all the banits needed was one word from their Lord. Then maybe all of them will leave to Amnus fortress. But no word, no sign, was showing.

Some of the elders came right near Efreu, so they can hear each other. One of them said, "Our Wise, please understand that we must fight for our homes, for our fortunes. What else we can fight for?"

"What else?! What else to fight for? Your soul. I say that is enough. The one who is killed by one of Voron's creatures will be lost forever. He will be touched by the sin, and he will have no chance to reach the eternal paradise. A city cannot give birth to new banits, but the banits can give birth to a new fortress!"

"We all know that your words speak the true. We agree that we must fight for our souls. But we'll fight from here. And by fighting here, we also protect our fortunes. Those who want to leave, so be it; but those who want to stay, they should stay."

The crowd was still yelling that they should prepare for the great fight.

"We are going to stay and protect our land," said the old man, showing the others elders that he wanted to stay.

"And I have to stay with you, my people, and try to defend the fortress. It's my duty."

When he heard these words, Efreu was destroyed. He expected such words from any of the voices but not from this voice. He turned back and saw that it really was the person who he hope will not be. It was Cafgar, his best friend for the last twenty years.

Efreu just looked at his friend.

"It's my duty," said Cafgar.

The wise left the room full of nerves. His powers were far exceeded. He knew that if many of the elders from Megros decided to stay, then many of banits will follow them. Also, their families, their relatives, their acquaintances, and many others will not leave them.

"Great Efreu," said a young man, "I will follow wherever you go. I'll do anything you say. Me, my family, my friends, and many others—we are going with you."

He was Emos, a young who was like Efreu's nephew.

"I know you will go with me, you and others, but I feel very bad for those who are staying. They are doomed, and they don't understand that."

For the first time Efreu was using his power God gave it to him. He rose up his scepter into the air and closed his eyes. There was a terrifying noise, the sound of thunder shaking everything around, even the buildings. Everyone stopped talking. Now Efreu can end his speech, "Tomorrow morning, we'll leave this town. Those who want—everyone who wants to leave should be prepared tomorrow morning because in dawn of the day we are leaving."

And he left.

The rest of the day everyone prepared himself. Those who were going to leave made their luggage, and the others put their armors and took their weapons. Those who were staying in Megros also rose up the barricade for the archers. They prepared big weapons for mass-kill; they boiled oil and all other things that should be prepared to defend their fortress.

This was the longest night for Efreu in his entire life. Maybe for everyone else, it was the same. Maybe some of them were sleeping like a baby. Some of them maybe weren't. Certainly it was that Efreu prayed all night.

Somebody had come at his door and knocked.

Efreu stood up from the rug on which he was kneeling and opened the door. It was Emos.

"Sorry to bother you, Great Efreu. But we have guests."

"Who came?"

"I don't know. Cafgar sent me to you." Those who came said that they were those who remained from the hordes and that they were coming from city of Mernas.

Efreu didn't say anything else. He ran outside.

It seemed that the forces of evil had already begun to attack anyone who didn't want to be their slaves, their soldiers. The "hordes," people from Marnas, had the same ancestors as the banits. But they were the people from the other side of the great river, from the old castle of Martos. But like the banits, the people from Marnas were the good people who escaped from the Lord of Light's anger. Those people were named Saemits or Marnasits—or the hordes people.

"Where are those from Marnas?" asked Efreu when he was near Cafgar. Cafgar was the leader of Megros, the most powerful banit, because of his huge fortune. He was the leader of the castle Megros, the army leader, because the spiritual leader was Efreu. Besides, he was the father of the most beautiful girl from that town. Her name was Adela.

Adela and Emos loved each other, but Cafgar stayed in the way of the two lovers. He was the one who always forbade Emos from meeting his daughter. For him what counted was not so much the love but the happiness of his daughter. But that was the problem.

He considered that his daughter deserved something better, and because of that, he was blinded. He didn't see that actually Emos would make her happy.

"They are at the west gate, Efreu. There are about one thousand men, women, and children. From what I heard, they are the only ones who escaped. The rest have perished under the sword of Night Lord and war. The evil army had not spared anyone. Absolutely nobody! The people from the hordes were almost decimated. And Marnas was destroyed. Everything turned into ruins. There is nothing there but death and destruction."

"At the west gate. It means that the forces of evil are everywhere. Those creatures that have attacked Aarnos and his brothers were in the south of the fortress."

"Maybe they are going to fight with Lord Voron against us. We should kill every one of them. Should I order my men to attack them?"

"No!" answered Efreu. "First we must speak with them. Let's go to the west gate then."

Outside everyone was prepared. Those who were able to fight—men, young, even some young boys and girls—were dressed in armor, some of them wearing helms, others without anything on their head. Everybody had a weapon. Each person who was willing to defend his family, relatives, and friends had at his thong one sword, one mace, or one axe. Some had bows. Some of them had one spear; others had a spear and a sword, two weapons, shields—everything that you needed for a war. Everybody who was strong enough was prepared to fight for his and his family's life. There were probably hundreds, maybe thousands, of such armed people. Those who were ready for leave the fortress and go to Amnus were almost two thousand. Those who remained to defend the castle from Megros were also many: over twelve thousand. Emos was among those who will leave, having one of his famous swords, made from the rarest material on their planet Zinusiul. Any weapon made from this material can cut any armor like in flesh. Unfortunately it was a metal very rare and very expensive. Emos, although he was a young wealthy man, couldn't afford to make many of such weapons. But even so, he managed to offer a few gifts to his close friends, one weapon for each. One of his friends, Billy, was near him just right now. The two were very good friends. Billy had a weapon made for his power. It was a huge mace; Emos made it especially for him. Three only-strong banits managed to lift that mace from the ground. But Billy was playing with him as Emos was playing with his sword.

Near Billy was his younger brother, named Rahanb. This name originated from the sacred language that meant "fighter" in banit. It was chosen by his parents for him because a few days after he was born a large hawk tried to take him from his mother's arms. But Rahnab held so tightly on his mother that he could not be kidnapped. He fought. When he grew up, the boy had to look up for his father's semues. Semue was some kind of cow but with huge horns. The boy always fought with the creatures that attacked his father's semues. He would sit on the semue, a huge cow with huge horns and every time would manage to send away the creature that attacked them. But we should all know that the creature that attacked them were not so dangerous.

Somewhere out was Hingus, another good friend of Emos but not one of Billy's friends. Hingus was a charming young man. He had the skin and hands like a woman's. He had long blond hair and blue eyes. Many girls had a crush on him. He was not like Billy. He was not only muscles. He was more like Emos, but because he didn't love any girl, like Emos did, you can say that he was more charming than the others. He knew how to charm almost all the young women. He often offered flowers and sweets to them. He even wrote poems for some of the young women. But like Emos and Billy, he knew how to fight well with his spears. Billy's brother, Rahnab, was the one who always carried Hingus's spears, because he got a lot of them. Also, Hingus is a good warrior. When he fought with someone for practice, Hingus often used to throw the spear when he had the chance. And even if the other warrior protected himself with the shield, almost all the time the other was a little bit hurt. Because Hingus threw the spear with such force, the shield made by wood was destroyed in many pieces. Once he managed to hit a target from two hundred meters away. And even if the target was so far, it also became lots of pieces.

He was the descendant of a noble's family. His family Ynoss was one of the richest families in Megros. Since the beginning, his family was already into trading. They bought the best products from other banits, kept those goods in stock buildings, and sold them after a while at much higher prices. They were very good tradesmen. They knew to sell any product, when to sell it, and how to make the buyer accept their prices.

So Hingus was a good-looking young man, a rich one, charming, and also a good fighter. All these were making him one of the most desired banits. And the young man knew this, so he was a little proud.

Because of his pride, there was a small rivalry between Aarnos and Hingus. Both were about the same age, both were attracted by the same young woman, Nuelle. And because Hingus had a great success while Aarnos was not so lucky, Aarnos hated everything about Hingus—at least so he said to Emos whenever they would speak. Something had to be about Hingus:

"I saw him again with Nuelle." He didn't have to say his name. Emos already knew about who they were going to speak about.

"Do not harm yourself. I do not believe there is something between them," Emos said. "They are just neighbors . . . nothing more."

"Easy for you to say. You love Adela, and she loves you more," told Aarnos to Emos. But these words only teased Emos. Billy did not know, but Emos would become sad every time he would hear the world knew about their love. They loved each other. But they could not be together because of her father's decision.

Because Emos said nothing, Billy continued, "Maybe she cares about me. Sometimes she smiles at me, but when I see how she laughs when Hingus tells her a joke—"

The most difficult was for Emos because he was a close friend to both. They were his best friends since childhood. Even if the three grew up together, in time Hingus and Billy became enemies. Maybe not quite enemies. But some tension was between them.

Both Billy and Hingus wanted to make each other learn a lesson. Both wanted to fight each other. For many years the two had confrontations, but they had never been beaten. Although Billy was much stronger, Hingus had dexterity and an incredible speed, so none of them had the courage to start a fight against the other. Many of those who were outside, heard what Efreu had said. Knowing that those from Mernas were at the castle gates, they hurried up to reach to the west gate. But Efreu and Cafgar, important personalities of fortress, had precedence. The others were held away by the soldiers who escorted Efreu and others from the elders, soldiers that also made a path between the tense crowds.

"Take us to master," said an incisive voice to the sentinel from the west gate. The one who spoke was a giant. The sentinel also had a rather large stature for a banit, but he scarcely came close to the giant's shoulder.

The one from the "horde" was dressed in a coat made from a beast fur, as big as him. Probably the coat was from one of those mythical creatures that really lived on Mania and which this giant had killed. It had a huge helm with two huge horns, which also came from a large animal. He also wore a huge mace. Everything that the giant from Marnas was wearing was huge.

The colossus's escort was composed by five other huge, some covered by a coat as grandiose as them, others with less. Perhaps in this way they may dignify the rank of those from the horde by the coat that was worn by each.

Six soldiers were at the gate. The others were a little behind. Their leader, plus five guards, had the courage to beat at the Megros's gates after more than four hundred years. In fact, they had never seen each other; only their ancestors had. But both sides, the banits and the horde, heard many stories about how their ancestors fought against each other. So nobody knew how this meeting will end. It's likely that the six would be able to beat easily fifty banits, but everyone can see that those from the horde were overwhelmed. Then why did they come here? They wanted to fight with the banits? Or perhaps they did not have any other option or did not know what else to do or who else to use.

Immediately when the banits saw that many strangers approached their town, more than several hundred of banits climbed the walls of the fortress with bows or spears. They were archers, marksmen, and others. However, they were in tough times. This visit was more unexpected than a little welcome.

Those from Marnas were so different of banits. They were much more massive compared to those who lived near the river Megros, which surround the Megros fortress. And their faces were like those of warriors. Some of them were really ugly, full of wounds and scars. The men of the horde had their canines like those of boars—fangs. So big were their canines that they could easily kill a banit with them. They looked so scary.

Only their women and their kids were a little bit nicer. They had smaller fangs.

The wounds of the "horde" were from battles or from the fights with creatures that lived on Mania, creatures they killed to procure those fur skins.

The sentinel replied, "More likely that my master does not want to see you. Those of Mernas are not well received here.

But he didn't finish his words, and someone cut him, "Open the doors!" sounded the voice of Efreu.

Frightened, the sentinel looked at Cafgar. The captain made a sign of approval.

"I hope you know what you're doing," whispered Cafgar to Efreu.

The sentinel also gave a sign to some soldiers, and the doors were opened. Those on the walls were terrified. If these warriors entering the castle had no thoughts of peace, they could easily kill many of the banits. Some of the elders went behind their guards, who were also very frightened.

Only Efreu, Cafgar, Emos, Billy, Hingus, and other brave men had remained to face the horde. Among them was Sindur with some of his men, ready to show how good of a soldier they were at any time. All of them were being prepared for any incident. The door opened hardly because of the weight. Nobody can destroy easily such a gate or cross on the other side of the walls easily. But now that the door was opened, who can tell what was going to happen?

Those who came from the lands of Mernas were so relieved when they entered the fortress of Megros. Even if they were a tribe of warriors, the men breathed a sigh of relief. The men tried to stop their tears. What they saw in their fortress, the force that nearly destroyed their race, which killed their brothers, sisters, parents, put so much fear in them, just as only the end of the world could.

The leader of the horde approached and spoke to Efreu, "My name is Shigash," said the leader with a handless and heavily language. "We come . . . Marnas City. Me klumb destroyed." He meant his fortress. "And everybody smashed," using his fist top hit his palm, showing how his friends and brothers were smashed by the evil army.

"I am Efreu. And he is Cafgar, one of the elders. He is the captain of the sentinels."

"We only survivors. Our klumb not anymore there . . . and was five times . . . bigger than this," spoke one from the horde.

Efreu was two times smaller than that colossus. And near him were only Emos, Aarnos, and Hingus, plus several other braves from Megros fortress. Those six from the horde could easily kill many of these banit soldiers. But even so, they stayed there to protect Efreu.

"How is it possible that such city was destroyed? It was five times bigger than this fortress. It had huge walls, and many of you seem to be incredible warriors," interfered Emos.

But he got no answer maybe because all the six from the horde were chieftains, and they only spoke with other leaders.

Efreu was very sad. What strength is born from the depth of darkness, which almost wiped off a race from the face of their lands? If that army decimated such warriors, how could the banits oppose it?

Shigash continued to speak to Efreu, "You no chance. No defend this small klumb. You doomed if stay here. You come with we."

"But surely you have destroyed a large part of the army who attacked you," said Sindur. Because he was one of those many who decided to stay and protect their castle and because he was one of the elders, he tried to increase the morale of his troops. Maybe in this way he will manage to make the others of his people to stay and fight for Megros.

"We almost no touch army evil but destroyed our Klumb. We only survivors." And he moved his arm all around, and he showed his tribe. Many of them were frightened. And they showed that. But their leader, Shigash, and other several people from the horde kept their fear inside.

"Hope there are survivors. Hope they escaped, hide behind high mountains." And he showed the great mountains.

The giant showed the direction of the Amnus castle. It looked like the Lord of Light somehow also showed them that only going there will give them a chance.

"We also prepare to go to the Amnus fortress. I talked with Michael. He said we should go straight toward those regions. You are welcome to accompany us and show us the way," said Efreu to Shigash.

These words made a lot of noise from the crowd. Everyone remained shocked by this news. Cafgar, Emos, and all others were stunned by Efreu's words. Those who wanted to remain respected the decision of the others. Also those who wanted to leave respected the decision of the others. But none of them didn't expect that those who were going to leave in this dangerous journey will travel through nowhere with the danger near them. The way the horde looked, their imposing stature, their ugliness—they were still a possible threat for the banits. They were not welcome to travel with the banits.

Almost all the banits that heard such words from Efreu became nervous.

"We don't want to be killed by them while we sleep!" said a voice, perhaps one of the elders.

"We won't travel with these creatures. We won't," said another.

"Maybe they were sent by Voron!"

"We made a mistake when we let them inside our fortress. Let's repair our mistake. Let's kill them!"

Such noise from the crowd, more yelling than a civilized discussion, made some soldiers from the horde's lines to come near Shigash and other leaders. They wanted to protect them from being killed.

"Look, they want to attack us!" said one from the elders, who was once a bloodthirsty soldier.

Every one stopped yelling. Over two hundred spear men went in front of their leaders and began to threaten the soldiers from the horde. More than a few hundred archers also threatened those from the horde. Theirs bows were extended at maximum. All of them waited just one word so the rain of arrows will hit those giants.

Also over fifty soldiers, who were now near their leaders, prepared their huge weapon to protect themselves. Upon seeing the huge swords, giant maces, great axes, those from the horde noticed the danger coming from the banits; so they began to retreat while the spear men considerably approached them.

All these happened in less than twenty seconds. The organized army of banits didn't need more than twenty seconds to regroup. The soldiers from the horde were very confused and scared. But still their faces were the faces of tough warriors.

"Wait! Wait!" yelled Efreu. "Don't harm them!"

He reached in front of the banits' army. Emos and Billy followed him. They tried to stop the spear men, but those two hundred soldiers continued to advance. Billy and Emos gave up when they saw that the soldiers didn't want to stop. They jumped away, but Efreu was still in danger. None of the elders said anything to stop the soldiers. None tried to protect Efreu.

"Stop!" yelled Efreu. But the army still approached him.

Efreu didn't say anything more. He rose his eyes to the sky, lifted his scepter, and whispered something. And when he hit the earth with his scepter, between him and the spear men, the earth cracked. And water began to flow through those cavities. This scared all the banits and the soldiers from the horde too. The archers let theirs bows down. Everything and everyone became calm. Even if the cavities weren't very large, you can cross between them; and even if the water wasn't so much, this little miracle stopped this attack, which could transform into something really terrifying.

"Master Efreu," said Sindur while he was approaching him. "I do not know if what you do—"

But Efreu made a sign for him to stop moving and speaking. He said, "All of you have the same face of war to wear! The hardest of the wars. All of must fight for our soul! We must fight for the souls of our children, and only if we do this together can we succeed!"

"But, master," Sindur tried to say something. But Efreu didn't let him to finish his words. "Even together we have few chances against these forces of evil! We had more than enough evil to face it. Don't start a fight one against the other because if we do so, we are lost from beginning."

"But the elders don't think that it is—" but once again he couldn't finish his words.

"The elders do not exist for me anymore! I won't listen whatever you have to say! If soon you let your men kill those soldiers and kill me, then make these people from the horde to be your brothers! None of you said anything! This was an inexcusable mistake!"

And he was looking at Sindur with such anger that the leader said nothing more, and he left. Very nervous, he took his soldiers and his close friends, almost all men from the elders, and he left. Only Cafgar and some of those who will leave the fortress Megros remained with Efreu, Emos, and Billy. Now Hingus and the other braves were also with them. They weren't there when the banits wanted to attack the horde, but when they heard about what happened, they came at the gates in a hurry. Who knows what else could happen?

After the banit soldiers left, Shigash and the other leaders came to Efreu. They bended a little bit as a sign of respect. Shigash said to Efreu, "Thank you stopping death of our children. We thought we lost. All of we—"

"We should fight together against the evil. Not one against the other," said the wise.

"The angel Kanah told us about you. He said we obey you. You're the one who talk to him. He said you know what to do." Kanah was Michael, and Ihtor was the name they gave to Gabriel.

"Michael is God's servant. He told me the God's will, and I tell to the others his commands. And he said that we have to face the hardest times, which have arrived. And he also said that our only escape is Amnus."

"We did same mistake. We tried stopping evil, but we almost lost all men. You see how we are." And Shigash showed again to Efreu what remained from his people.

And he continued, "My advise you to leave. You no chance destroy evil from here. Me advise all of you. Leave!"

"We'll leave right away."

And he turned around looking to the crowd and yelled so anyone can hear him, "We leave in two hours! Everyone is welcome to join us! Our brothers from the horde are coming with us too. Take only foods and weapons! And be careful. Maybe there are lots of evil soldiers outside!"

"And this is not only danger. We must be prepared. Lots of dangers out there. Lots of dangers in journey . . . very dangerous."

Efreu looked at Shigash. What was the giant trying to say? What was the meaning of his words? Mania was a big planet. It could hide lots of threats. But could those threats scare such a giant warrior, like Shigash? The ancestors said that Voron, "master of darkness," sometimes let his beasts on Mania so they can feed on fresh meat. But the banits didn't meet those creatures. They didn't venture into foreign lands and deep forests and didn't climb mountains or hills. They frequented only those places familiar for them. The rest of the lands were forbidden for them. Only some of the elders, three or four, had seen such creatures. But maybe those were only stories," thought everyone a few days ago. These were stories about animals higher than ten banits, about a giant creature flying in the high of heaven, probably to procure food.

But now Efreu and the others heard those words from Shigash. So there must be some truth to those stories.

He said nothing to Shigash. He looked at the crowd. The crowd was petrified because of all that happened. Many of them were terrorized. Nobody was moving. Many of them were also nervous. They didn't like the idea of traveling with those from the horde.

"Don't stay here in front of me! Time is precious! Go and prepare yourself! We'll meet at the east gate! In two hours we leave!"

And so, a lot of banits spread away to prepare. Those who will leave Megros to go to fortress Amnus went to prepare for the journey, taking all that was needed for a long and difficult journey through the desert. Those who will fight to defend their fortress Megros went to take their armors and weapons, and they made all the preparation to defend their city. But many of those soldiers who were going to try defending this fortress send away their family. They had to remain because it was their duty, but their family had to go. They didn't have to stay and die.

Great simmer in Megros fortress. Many soldiers were dressed in armors with shields and many weapons. All were ready to give their life to defend the castle. All army was focused at the west gate, which led to the fortress ruins of Marnas, where the horde came from.

Cafgar also wore an armor, armed with one sword. Adela was there, Cafgar's wife, and his three-year-old son. Adela and his wife were crying. The little boy did not really know what was happening, but he was crying because of the noise. Cafgar's wife was trying to stop her tears. She tried to make her son to stop crying too. But she had no success in doing this.

"Please come with us," said the wife.

Cafgar looked at his daughter. Adela could not say anything. She was only crying.

"I cannot let my people—I must stay with them. I must protect those innocent women and children who are going to remain into Megros."

The two women began to cry harder. Now they knew that there was no chance for them to see Cafgar leaving. He won't come with them.

"But you should certainly go to the Amnus."

Emos was nearby. He knew that Adela, her mother, and her brother will go to castle Amnus; he wanted to be close to them into this long journey. In that crowd of over twenty thousand people, hardly could he find them, so he better stayed near them.

Cafgar saw the young, although Emos tried to hide, and he made a sign to the boy to approach. Emos came.

"Young man, I know that we don't understand well. And it was my entire fault. But from now on, I want to understand that you love my daughter and that she loves you too. And that you deserve to be with her. I was blind. I didn't understand that you respect my daughter like none does. That you love her and you will protect her better even than me."

He looked at Emos for the first time with gentleness. In the past, every time he had met the boy, he looked at him with such anger. He knew that Adela has been meeting Emos in secret. And he could never do anything against it. He tried to discuss with her daughter; he tried to tell her that she needed a husband from a noble family, not a warrior.

But now he understood that all the time he was against their happiness. Maybe you'll think that it doesn't matter anymore. Maybe you think that they won't live enough to recover the lost time, and maybe it's true. But what I can tell you is that true love lasts forever. Even after death.

The young said nothing, so Cafgar continued, "To fix all my mistakes, I give you my blessing. If Adela loves you and she wants to be your wife, then nothing can stand in your way. Not even me. Not even death."

He looked at his family; he kissed his boy on the cheek, and he continued to speak, "But please do something for me." And he looked once again to Adela. "From now on, Adela will follow you. And maybe she'll be your wife. And from that moment, she will be your mother, and he will be your brother. From that moment, it will be your duty to protect them. Even with the price of your life. You must promise me that you will be so. Promise me!"

Some tears flowed easily on Cafgar's cheek. And a deep sadness was showing his face. His heart was wrought because of the idea that maybe it's the last time he will see his family. Last time to hear their voices.

"I promise," said Emos. "My life is less important than their lives. I will do my best to protect them. And also my friends will do the same. And so I will do for their families."

When he heard these words, Cafgar's face became a little lighter. He knew that Emos was a good warrior, and he also knew that he will do everything to protect his family and other banits.

"Please come with us," said Adela to his father once again.

But Cafgar touched her gently and said, "You'll see that everything will be fine. In few days, after we destroy the evil force, somebody will come to you. And he will tell you that we won the battle. And you will return in Megros, and everything will be fine once again, like in the old days."

And he left them. He took the soldiers over his command and disappeared into the crowd. Slowly, slowly, those who went to the east gate leave to Amnus got out. The long and dangerous journey they would have to make had begun. A journey full of dangers, full of risks.

When he approached the gates, Cafgar saw a sea of men. Lots of soldiers. He was pleased that the elders finally understood that it's better to send their families away. Even if those families didn't leave with the others, children, old people, and women of those who didn't want to let their families with the horde were escorted by five hundred soldiers. They will hide themselves into some caves not very far from Megros. In two days they will be in those caves.

So the number of soldiers that were going to defend the castle was smaller with five hundred thousand, only five thousand soldiers, but they were going to do everything to get a defensive position as well, with bows, spears, or other throwing weapons. They also had swords for the event of a siege from their enemy; the enemies could easily climb the walls of the fortress with some ladders.

They had strengthened the gates with all kinds of huge logs, strutted into the gate with one tag and with the other extremity deep into the ground. Many banits were down near the gate. The best fighters—most powerful, brave, and skillful in handling arms—were down at the gate, ready to face against the enemy.

The fortress was surrounded almost everywhere by water. So they could protect their homes easily than those from the horde did. Or at least this is what those from Megros thought.

The most vulnerable place in this city was the gateway from the west. The gate was probably the direction where from the invaders will make their appearance. The other two gates, those from the south and north, were used only by small fishing boats. Crossing through the two gates, you can find two little docks for only ten to fifteen boats each. The gate from the east, the one through which the others had left, had a long and strong bridge. The bridge was over five hundred meters high and built from strong rocks. On the left and right side of that bridge was water. And the bridge's width was only five to ten meters.

So the only gate you could attack was the one from the west. But to do this, you have to kill the soldiers who stood on those high walls, but they were very well hidden in their places.

Lots of people were at the west gate. Norus was there too, surrounded by his servants to protect him from the army of death. His armor was more brilliant, with precious stones, and better worked than the other armors. The most beautiful armor was Norus's. The others had shields and armor of all kinds and all sizes. The wealthy people had new armors, and the poor had used armors.

However, this matter was too little to them. All people were concerned about the fight they will face very soon. Everyone tried to barricade the fortress as best as he can. Some had formed barricade on their buildings. Because the walls could not hold so many people, some of the banits had made outposts on the roofs of their houses. The banits stood together ready to fight until death will take them. They were ready to defend this city and their families. Everyone who was able to fight was spread everywhere around the west gate. After this gate and these walls, there was an area with a large surface where the banit swordsmen, axe men, mace men, and all the other soldiers will face the enemy. More than twenty thousand soldiers could stay in that plaza. Five thousand banits and another fifteen thousand soldiers could fight there. But let's hope that the evil army won't send so many soldiers because if it will be so, then the banits had no chance of winning the battle

Cafgar gave some orders to some archers and spearmen to climb up on places in the walls, there where he thought there should be more soldiers. Norus and other leaders also gave orders to other soldiers. Besides the fact that they had lots of money, Norus and those from the elders had a lot of experience in battle. They were good strategists. So the banits listened to everything they had said. Cafgar saw that everyone was prepared. All soldiers had a defensive position, the best they could take. Armed with swords and bows, some had big rocks near them. They will use it to smash their enemy. They also had many bottles with hot oil. Everyone was prepared to fight against the army of death. Everyone who could fight against Voron had a weapon, a shield, and an armor. Even the young boys were wearing armors and weapons.

"It's time to show that you will die for your brothers and sisters!" said Cafgar. "To show how brave and strong you are! It's time to sacrifice our life for our children if it has to be so. For them, we'll do all this. But remember. Even if after this battle you'll go into the eternal lands, your name will be spoken by your children with honor."

Everyone was so quiet after Cafgar spoke. It was a quiet evening; not even one little animal made any noise. Not even one insect. Nothing. All the soldiers were terrified. None of them could say anything. It's so a repressively quiet, just like in a graveyard.

But everything was so light. The two months which are around Mania light enough this area which would be a battleground.

Now Cafgar was thinking about something. Maybe he was thinking at what is going to happen in the next future. About this terrified battle. He thought that probably it was not the best choice when they decided to defend the fortress Megros, but many of these men were quite experienced fighters. Cafgar was in the front of the soldiers. He and some others from the elders, surrounded by many braves, were going to face the evil army in first line. Even if there were many people who could defend the gate and they could stand in back to protect themselves, they hadn't done so. They were brave men. They wanted to save the Megros fortress out of the hands of those who could make it become ruins. It's true that some men from the elders, which once in past fight themselves in chest that they care for Megros more than others, were a little behind, but this doesn't matter too much in these moments. Certainly is that those who could fight, and even more than that, even young boys and some girls, were there to fight.

"You've stayed here, and you said that you want to defend the fortress! But I tell you. This battle is for protecting your families! They can live without this castle. But the castle couldn't live without them."

These words probably motivated all the soldiers. Or probably not. But it is certain that they yelled so strong that the walls almost shook. Five thousand men, brave soldiers, made such noise that you can't even imagine.

"So fight for our families! And protect this city as best as you can for them." But this time nobody heard Cafgar. All the soldiers yelled and hit the swords by their shields, a sound heard miles away. Maybe even the enemies heard it.

"Only five thousand men against the unknown," said Cafgar to himself because none of the others can hear him in that noise.

But he smiled when he saw all those strong soldiers who are ready to fight for their families until death will take them.

"Maybe we a have a chance," he said.

The army of death, the "house of the dead," like what the Holy Book spoke about Voron's army, was left on Mania to attack the banits when the angel of God blew into his trumpet, a sign that showed that the end was near. Anyone who will manage to live from this war will have a chance to reach to the lands of eternal, to be a fighter of justice, a servant of the Creator. But not so many reached there because Voron, from what Efreu and other prophets predicted many years ago, had created a huge and diverse army to destroy everything, which was right and everyone who followed God's will. And all this will happen or had happened not only on Mania but on other planets too. Who knows when all this will happen on Earth because it is certain that it will happen.

Few hours passed since everything was prepared for castle defense. And in almost three hours the night will pass. Maybe there it won't be a battle. Maybe the force of evil is not so strong.

You can hear nothing. Not even an insect. Nothing. For almost one hour. But one hour ago some terrified roars were heard deep into the forests, which were near the castle's gates. Only five hundred meters were between the fortress walls and forest. And the trees, called imensialiss, were more than seventy meters high.

LAST BATTLE *for* MANIA

And the treetop of imensialiss was so thickset that you can see nothing through it. Those roars were so close. The banits knew that the danger was close to them. But they can't see anything. Because of that, everyone from the walls was stunned when they heard those sounds. None of them knew what that could be. But it was certain that it was one big monster. A very big one. Let's hope that there won't be more of them.

But suddenly the deep silence ended. Lots of movement and lots of fuss were heard from the woods; some shadows loomed from the forest. It could easily see that those soldiers from the army of death were eager to attack and destroy the banits. But something stopped them.

"There are no catapults or other mechanisms of assault. It will be hard for them to break Megros's walls," said a voice from the wall. It was one of the soldiers.

Those who were waiting down to fight against the evil army after the walls will be broken became more confident of their strength. The fact that the aggressors didn't have machines to help them in the siege of this fortress was a good thing. The banits were a little calmer now. Without some high stairs, without some catapults to destroy the walls, without a battering ram to destroy the gate, the siege will be quite difficult for the aggressors. Maybe even they won't attack the fortress when they will see that they will have no chance. Or maybe after a little battle, after those from the evil army will lose many soldiers, they will see that they have no chance of victory so they will leave.

Almost every banit from Megros thought that it will be an easy battle. A victory for them. Maybe it will be so. Maybe.

But suddenly another soldier from those walls said, "It is something down there! Some huge creatures . . . they are in groups. I think they want to throw something into our walls! But what are those huge creatures? Is it possible?".

But he didn't finish talking, and big pieces from Megros walls were flying everywhere. The banits were also flying away like bugs. Tens of banits were thrown from the walls and buried under the pieces of broken walls. A huge piece of the wall rolled away, taking another several tens of banits with it. When he stopped, it also smashed and buried others of banits. A rain of arrows came from the sky above the banits from outside—and all these in one minute. An aggressive and terrifying attack came over the banits.

The banits tried to answer to the attack from the walls too. Many of them were shooting arrows, others were throwing javelins, and others were prepared to disgorge hot oil.

The banits were terrified. The aggressors didn't have siege machines. "What happened?" thought everyone. Those from the walls said that they didn't saw any siege machines, but still the wall was broken. What they didn't know was that the army of death was always well prepared. They had some huge monsters, more than fifteen meters in high, which can throw huge rocks long distance away. And what they had thrown was some kind of metal sphere with awns, which also had some liquid inside them. And when those huge spheres were hitting the walls, a huge explosion destroyed everything around.

So now huge holes were into the walls.

Many brave men were immediately at those holes, ready to fight with those who dared to enter into the fortress. But even if they were very brave, you can see on their faces that they were terrified because of the roars.

Those most horrid sounds came closer and closer, and those braves were more terrified than ever, although they were prepared to give their life in this battle. They couldn't see anything, so they didn't know against what they had to face, but it was certain that the aggressors were very, very strong.

Cafgar was also scared to death, but he remained in the front line, close to the gate.

"Wait!" called Cafgar for some of those banits who got out to face the enemy. "Don't break the lines. We have to stay together. It is certain that those who got outside died in the moment when they were outside the walls because there were moments when rains of arrows came from the aggressors. And those arrows were rejected only because the banits remained together. Those who broke the lines couldn't face to such a rain of arrows."

Even if Cafgar and other strategists yelled to their people not to go out, some of the banits continued to get out.

"Don't break the line! Don't break the line!" yelled many good warriors to the men from their commands.

Cafgar also yelled to his men to stay in the lines. He looked again to those banits who were still on the walls. Not so many of them remained. The rains of arrows harvested many of them. Good soldiers, good people—many of them also came down because they had better chance of surviving in one front-to-front battle.

But like I said, many of those who were still on what remained from the walls were still or could be harvested by arrows. Cafgar could see all these in front of his eyes. He also could see how some parts of the walls had fallen because of their weight or because they were hit be other spheres.

Suddenly one terrified sound was heard close the gate, the roar of one beast ready to kill his prey, and after that, those who were close to the gate heard a slam and saw how the gate became pieces. Those pieces from the gate and from the logs strutted to hold the gate hit some banits.

Cafgar got rid of those pieces of wood that could easily kill any of them. He protected himself with his shield. And without fear, he moved toward the gate to receive what was behind it.

While he was moving toward the gate, two soldiers from the evil forces had entered the gate. They were dressed in armor, and one of them had a cudgel with many nails caught in it. The other had a mace. They had the size of a banit. Only that their body was more bones with some skin and meat on them. In some places, on their faces and bodies, where the armor didn't hide their corpus, you can see only dry bones. The meat was missing almost entirely; there was only dry skin hiding the bones of the face. Those creatures named "sahtari" by the ancestors and by the banits were some kind of dead mummies.

The two swooped to Cafgar because he was the first soldier they had to face after they had got through the walls. And when they approached him, they tried to strike him; but Cafgar, a true warrior, avoided the dangerous weapons of the sahtari, and he hit those two creatures with such power that he threw them down. Right behind Cafgar were his brave men who were ready to give up their life. Sounds of courage you can hear from their mouth, and those sounds made the banits from behind to get courage and to throw themselves in to the battle. When he looked back to his soldiers, Cafgar got some divine power from his heart, and his courage grew more.

But when he turned his eyes to the place where the gate was, he saw a horrible creature inside the fortress. That creature had a double-edged huge axe and an armor covering his chest, arms and legs. But the armor from his legs and arms had the capability to let him move easily. His shield was on the left arm, on his elbow area. The face of the monster was not covered. Cafgar could easily see that the creature was a bull that blew strong air from his nostrils, a sign showing he was very angry and dangerous. The banits called this creature an "hralf," a creature born from sins.

Even if he was scared, Cafgar ran to face that creature. And when he was almost three meters away, he prepared his sword, and he tried to hit it with all the strength he had. But the hralf also prepared his axe to protect himself. When the two weapons touched each other—because of the strength of the monster, which was more than six times stronger than Cafgar's—he banit was thrown away twenty meters. He his body on a building's wall with such power that Cafgar couldn't stand up. He only saw more and more hralfs inside his fortress, hitting the banits with such strength that none could face them. And more and more "sahtari" filled up the area where the fight was. Sahtari with maces, swords, cudgels, or other weapon of this kind and sahtari with a mantle over their armor and some kind of crown, maybe leaders, with some staffs spitting fire from their top. Those leaders were followed by the sahtari soldiers.

Cafgar also saw how the walls became ruins. Now he knew that the fortress Megros had lost. They have no chance to protect it. He could see once more many hundreds—thousands—of soldiers from the evil army entering the fortress. And then everything

around him became darker, and hardly could he hear the noise of the battle. He could only whisper, "We lost"
And so was Cafgar too.

From the high of heaven, you could see several thousand people of banits and marnasits. They were moving as quickly as they can to reach to Amnus, their only escape.

Even if the distance between the travelers and Megros was almost one day away, the banits and those from the "horde" going to Amnus could hear the sounds of the battle. Sounds of destruction and chaos, sounds of perdition.

Women and children were abandoned to despair, and they were crying. Mothers were trying to relieve their children, but the evil was everywhere in the air, so they were not leaving in peace. Men were also scared. But they could not leave their desperation to forestall them. They should at least not show their fear. If this happens, everything is lost. And they couldn't afford it. Their families were all they still have. Everything left from the two tribes were now moving toward their only escape: the fortress of light and peace, the fortress Amnus.

Twenty miles away, before that crowd, were Efreu, Emos, Shigash, Billy, Hingus, and other brave men. There were fifteen banits and the other four leaders from the horde. Those fifteen banits maybe weren't so good a fighter as our heroes, but certainly they were fearless. Shigash also took his best warriors. What can I say about them? You'll never see so good a fighter like them. Only those from God's army were better fighters.

This group's task was to go ahead and release the way from any danger so the women, elders, and children won't be hurt from any unknown danger. Efreu knew that the evil army wasn't the only danger they had to face.

The banits and those from the horde were still watching each other. The banits didn't have full confidence in those strong warriors, and those from the horde were also looking out for their safety. Even if all of them were listening Efreu, they didn't like each other. Only a spark was all they need to fight against each other.

But even so, Billy was looking with admiration at those warriors. Billy was so big, so strong, but those soldiers looked stronger. "Can I beat such a warrior?" thought Billy. "Look at those skins. So great creatures have those animals been. But they killed them." All five warriors were covered with some unknown skins; they had wounds on the body, and their arms and legs weren't covered. So you can see that their muscles and their strong shoulder could face five banits easily.

Emos approached Efreu. He had some questions for the wise, "Great Efreu."

The old man looked at Emos.

"Can you tell us how long the way to the castle Amnus is?"

"In eleven days we will be there. And the others will arrive a day after us. That is if everything will be fine, and we don't have to face any danger."

"But aren't the soldiers of Voron reaching us? Or worse is it possible to reach those who are behind us?"

"No, they are waiting for Voron. And they are waiting for the knight kings . . . They will set their camp in Megros. Only one week after he'll reach Amnus they will be there with all the army. And Voron will be there too."

Efreu chilled when he pronounced that word. Voron—this was only a simple word, but it meant strength not even God could kill it forever. A strength that was becoming stronger every day, strength like no other.

But Emos didn't see Efreu's trembling. He was concerned by the other words. Emos bowed his head, and he said with half of voice to Efreu, "So those who stayed to fight in Megros . . . they—"

But he stopped talking. He couldn't say that word.

"Yes, they are lost," said Efreu to complete his phrase.

A short pause came into this dialogue. There was a short moment of silence for those who once were their brothers, relatives, and neighbors.

"I'm very sorry for them. If only they accepted to come with us."

"They should know that we couldn't face such an army without God's help. And maybe some of them knew that. Maybe they—"

But Efreu didn't finish his words. Not far from them, into the deep forest, he heard some powerful roars. Sounds came from everywhere, but those were strong roars. The entire group heard those sounds. They stopped and prepared to fight against anything that can attack them. But the roars became quickly more and more slowly. Whatever it was now running away. The group began to advance again.

"But now we must be concerned about those who come behind us. They are everything we still have."

"Let's hope that the evil army will need some time to get together. We'll have time to prepare ourselves for the battle."

"Only if we won't have to face the dangers that our way is hiding from us." And all these being said, our group of heroes disappeared into the deep forest of imensialiss.

"You heard that?"

A powerful sound of a river could be heard from the place where the banits were.

"Such a lovely sound! Fresh water," said Aarnos. "This has to be fresh water, very good to satisfy our thirst. We should hurry up a little bit."

The banits began to run toward the place from where they heard the water flowing.

"Wait!" said a loud voice. The banits stopped running. Shigash was the one who spoke. He continued, "Where there is water, there are also creatures who drink from that water. It would be better to stick together."

But how can they listen to somebody they didn't trust enough? The banits didn't care about the warrior's words. They ran away through that water with Billy and Hingus in front of the group.

Shigash made a sign to Efreu showing that they had to follow the banits and stop them. But the banits were running faster than the others because Efreu was not moving so fast, and they had to wait for him.

Billy, Hingus, and the banits were stunned by the beauty of the forest. They saw small animals running away scared because of the noise the group made. Birds were singing beautifully, and the sound of falling water made everything so magical. Even if the fortress Megros was so close to the imensialiss forest, the banits never entered so deep like they did now. Only their ancestors hundreds years ago had that courage. But because many of them didn't return back, they disappeared; the banits' ancestors decided not to go into the forest near Megros anymore. So after many, many years, all those journeys of the ancestors became stories, which were more or less entirely true. They were the first banits who discovered these unknown beauties: animals they never saw, plants and fruits they never tasted, and birds with songs they never heard.

The banits were closer and closer by that sound of water, which took their minds. After almost a day of running through the desert, they found this forest. The coolness of the forest offered them what they needed after more than 10 hours into the heat. But now the sound of the water called them. And they needed this more than anything in this moment. So the banits were in hurry to find that place with water. Those from the horde, the marnasits, came just after them. But while they advanced into the forest, they looked everyplace to assure that there was nothing that could attack them. They even looked behind.

With them were Efreu and Emos. Because of his age, Efreu couldn't advance so quickly. Also the wise was watching every corner of the forest. With his staff in his right hand, the prophet was moving slowly through the forest. His only weapon was that staff. He had no armor like the others or any helmet or shields. For him that staff was his weapon and armor. But he can use that staff only against Voron's army.

"'You can't use it against my creation. You can use it only against evil,' that's what my Lord told me," said Gabriel to Efreu when he gave the staff to him.

"But how can I tell if they are evil or not those who will attack me?"

"It will show you."

That discussion between Efreu and Gabriel was many years ago. And all he did by now with that staff were little miracles or things like he did when the banits and the marnasits had argued. Since then Efreu could never use the true power of God. That weapon was brought by the divine power.

"Look! It's such an incredible view," said Billy. And so it was. From some high rocks, the water was falling down into the lake. But the waters fell with such power that when it reached down, it touched some big rocks, which got out from the lake, forming an incredible rainbow over that lake. All those colors—combined with the strong green of the forest, with the blue of the water, with the red, pink, yellow, and many others colors from the flowers near the lake—hypnotized anybody. Anybody besides those from the horde.

The marnasits were looking at something less attractive than all those colors. The lake was once part of the forest. You can see that because of the trees that were out from the water. There was an interesting view, but this thing also didn't have the marnasits' attention. They were looking at some thrown trees. Something or someone threw them all with the roots, and everywhere around those trees were wood particles.

"Something is wrong with these," said Shigash.

But just before he finished what he had to say, the birds began to fly through the sky, and no other little creature didn't show. All these because of one powerful roar. None of the banits knew what that creature was, but certainly those from the horde knew because using their claws they climbed up the imensialiss trees in few seconds, and they disappeared immediately into the tree's crowns.

"Those are csilias. They like meat. Hit the creature in the head. Your arrow and swords have no effect against his body," said Shigash. "And keep the creature into the forest."

And he also disappeared.

It's a good idea to keep it into the forest because the creature was almost five times higher than a marnasit, so he could hardly run after the banits through the trees. The banits saw it coming toward them.

"Let's go toward the lake! But don't get out of the woods. Stay under the trees!" yelled Efreu.

The group increasingly moved toward the lake.

"Watch out the water. Water can also hide danger!"

"We shouldn't trust those cowards," said Billy to the others.

Efreu looked at him and said, "Surely they have a reason."

"Yes! They tried to save their head. This is a good reason," Billy answered ironically.

"Target the head of the beast!" Efreu told the banits. "Do as the marnasits said!"

The beast was closer and closer. Now the banits could see that it was some sort of a giant, with some huge arms. These arms had three fingers each and with some long claws, almost half of a banit each. Those claws were strong and curved just like some swords. Probably they were the main weapons of the creature, used to kill the prey and make it into small pieces, so he could eat it.

A brown fur covered all of the creature's body. On his neck and head, he was covered by a more thickset and longer fur. It was five times higher than a marnasit, but certainly over ten times more powerful. While he was running after the banits, he swept away everything in front of him. His mouth was also very scary. His fangs were so huge that easily he would be able to break a banit in two pieces.

The creature felt the strange smell of the banits, those strangers who dared to enter in his forest. But now that he could see them, he became extremely agitated. He ran just through the banits when he was near them. It moved so fast. He threw his arms with those long claws, but he didn't manage to catch anyone. The banits jumped away to save their lives and began to fire arrows against the creature.

But the creature returned toward the group. And this time one of them was not so lucky. The beast stabbed him. The claws easily penetrated the banit's armor and got through his body. The poor man could just scream when the powerful beast hurt him. A moment after that, he was thrown away by the monster. The banit and the others will be the monster's dinner.

Devastated and angry because the creature killed one of them, Hingus took a spear and threw it directly into the neck's creature. The beast became dizzy because of the powerful hit. Lucky for him that his body found a tree in his way to sustain the weight of his body. Else, maybe he would fall down, and hardly could such a creature stand up when it is hurt.

After the creature recovered his stability, he pounced toward Hingus.

Poor Hingus was doomed. Even his spear could not do anything to kill that thing. The banits continued to fire arrows on the head of this monster. But the fur was very long in that area of the head. And so the arrows that had managed to reach in this area of the beast's head fell down or remain hanging into the dense hair. Just a few hit the target and managed to touch the creature, but it only pissed the creature harder; it can't hurt him seriously. Hingus's spear was the only weapon that succeeded to hurt the monster seriously. The banits could see how blood flowed from the head of the beast. But it was not enough to beat him. And now poor Hingus, one of the best warriors of the banits, will have the same tragic end like the other had.

The beast began to run after Hingus. Those roars were so terrifying. Hingus was stunned when he saw that the creature was attacking him. He couldn't do anything. The creature was moving closer and closer to Hingus, ready to kill the banit.

But when it was almost near Hingus, from one tree, somebody jumped on the back head of the creature. A very large axe hit the creature on top of his head with such power that you hear the sound of a skull bones being crushed. A load roar of pain sounded from the creature's mouth; then the beast fell down. And the warrior who killed that beast jumped from it just before the creature touched the earth. Without any scratch on him, he said to the banits, "Told you to aim the head," and he smiled.

He was Shigash, the great warrior. This brave soldier who knew almost every creature that ran through the woods or through the desert of Mania, killed the beast so easily.

But there were some creatures he didn't meet until now.

When he saw the body of the dead banit, he stopped smiling. He continued to say, "Looks like we came late."

The others also jumped so easily from the trees. They jumped between the trees to succeed in jumping on the head of that creature. The one who succeeded that better than the others was Shigash. But this didn't mean that the others didn't do anything. They worked as a team. And the one who killed the beast was Shigash because he was closer of that csillias.

"I thought you ran," said Efreu to the giant.

"A member from the horde not running any danger. Especially when the danger attack friends. You did let us come with you in Amnus. So our duty to protect you."

"We are very happy to have you as allies . . . and very grateful," said Efreu with the due respect for the one who saved their lives. It could be worse than it is. More of us could be dead because of that creature. And that could be worse not only for us but also for those who were behind us. "Our wives and children, thank you for saving our lives."

"Pleasure is for Shigash," smiled the giant again.

It looked like the marnasits were braver than the banit soldiers. Even the huge Billy, who had almost the same size like Shigash had, couldn't do anything to help the banits. That was because even if he had the strength of five banits, he couldn't jump between the trees like those from the horde could, and he also didn't know anything about how to kill such creatures. Actually he didn't know anything about killing them.

Proof besides their clothes which are made from all kind of creature skins, besides theirs great size and theirs warrior's looks, beside all that, now even their facts show that the marnasits are great warriors. And if at the beginning when they first met, between the banits and the marnasits it was some kind of a dispute, now they are all friends. Maybe they still weren't entirely very good friends, but it was certain that those tensions at the beginning were gone. Even Billy, the one who was skeptic about traveling with those from the horde, when the four marnasits got down from the trees he stretched his arm to one of the marnasits. He stretched his arm to Marnuk, another great warrior but a character as stubborn as Billy. Marnuk saw the banits as incapable people. The banits couldn't live if they won't be near, to help them. And perhaps it was true. Even there were three times more banits than marnasits, the people from Megros couldn't kill that creature, which the marnasits could kill so easily. So Marnuk considered that the banits were little powerless people. Good warrior it's true, but this wouldn't help them in this world where you need strength.

But he had some kind of respect for Billy. He knew that Billy was extremely strong. When he was in one tree, he saw indeed an action full of courage from the banit. He saw how Billy hit with such power in that creature that the beast yelled. Even if he hit the creature on its back, which was not a weak area because it had petrified skin there, the beast felt Billy's painful coup. And even if the hit didn't make any wound on the beast, the creature staggered a little bit, and it also howled.

The two shook hands, binding a close friendship between two races, banits and the marnasits, that kind of friendship needed in such moments.

The two began to speak about everything. Billy asked the warrior many questions about the creatures he killed. There were many creatures—a lot to speak about.

While they were speaking, the others were looking at the beast. It was huge. One of Shigash's men took a knife and began to flay the skin from the dead creature. Two banits were helping him. The marnasit showed them which parts they should take, and they also began to flay the beast. It was similar to the skins the hordes were wearing. It was better than an armor and more easily worn but with toughness that the banits were not used of.

The skin of the dead monster was very easy to model into a body of a person once you began to cut from the head. But if you try to cut with a sword or anything else from the outside, surely you'll fail. The horde was wearing such furs because these were the best shield they knew.

The others watched how the three were working. Some of them talked about the creature's size; some settled on the dry leaves around those three. Even Emos, Hingus, and Aarnos were looking at that creature.

But as usual, Shigash was watching. Even if he was speaking with Efreu about what they had to do next, his eyes ran in every corner of that wood.

Suddenly he stopped speaking. It was too quiet. No creature, no bird, no sound. What could have happened? The creature that could attack or scare them was dead.

"Hear that?" said Shigash to Efreu.

"What? I don't hear anything."

"Yes," answered the giant.

Then he looked very carefully deep into the forest. Where they were now, near that lake, into that glade, they could be in danger. Any monster could see and attack them. But the problem was that no creature ran through the woods. No bird on trees.

"Something happened," said Shigash loud enough so anyone can hear him.

Efreu watched him, a little scared. The marnasit was very nervous. He looked everywhere, but he can't see anything. "What can it be?" he asked himself.

Suddenly yelled to all, "Something in the water!"

And he was so right. But it was too late for them. Some creature, some kind of a huge snake, caught the marnasit flaying the skin of the csillias. He dragged him into the water as quickly as he got out, and nobody could help the marnasit. He was lost.

"Away from the water!" screamed Shigash to the others.

Then three more snakes, which looked just like the first one, got out from the water, trying to kill the others. Two of them didn't manage to catch any prey, but one had luck. It caught one of the banits. But when he tried to drag him into the water, Billy hit the creature with his axe with such power that he almost cut the head of that snake.

A terrified howl got out from the creature's mouth. All the water wavered from where the snakes got out. When the water was beginning to boil, the snake dropped the banit. But even if he was hurt, he managed to run toward the others, and the snake disappeared into the water.

Another two snakes got out. But they didn't attack anybody. They were looking to Billy, and from their looks, you can understand that they will attack Billy. The other two snakes were also setting their eyes on Billy. All the snakes were preparing to attack him, probably to revenge the other. It was certain that the other was dead; you can see that from the blood from the water. And no creature can survive from such an attack.

Now four terrible snakes were going to attack Billy. No, five. Another one got out from the water. And now five snakes were ready to kill Billy. And nobody was near to help him. Suddenly the battle was beginning. Two of the snakes attacked Billy almost the same time. The giant succeeded to avoid the creatures, and even he managed to hurt one of them. But the other, just after he hurt one snake, managed to take Billy's axe. And now, the other snakes were ready to attack him. And they did so.

But just before they can catch Billy, a huge axe was flying just like a boomerang in the air, hurting two of the snakes.

Marnuk was the one who was closer to that creature, and he managed to throw his weapon toward those snakes. Lucky for him he managed to hit his target, and probably, he saved Billy's life. But unlucky for Marnuk, the last snake got him because he was too close by the lake.

The banits began to hit those snakes with arrows. Hingus and those from the horde threw some spears. With such power from Hingus, his spears got through one snake's body. But even so the creature could fight against the group.

Because the banits and the marnasits came too close by water, other two banits were caught by snakes. Too much easy. Something was not right. It looked like the snakes were working as a team. Even if one snake didn't manage to catch a prey, other snake came from another angle, and it succeeded to catch someone.

And now Marnuk was in the air in one snake's mouth, one banit was dragged in the water, the other was trying to escape from the pinch of one snake, and Billy also was caught by his leg. Emos was fighting with the snakes to protect and to release his friend, but the snakes attacked the banits one after the other.

"Stop trying to attack him! It's not a snake!" yelled Efreu. "It is a hynd, a creature with multiple heads! And there is no way to kill it even with an army. Run from it! Run from the lake! Use your arrows and spears to attack the beast!"

All were frightened but were eager for revenge at the same time. Soon they understood that they had no chance against such creature. Even the marnastis never saw such beast.

Efreu couldn't help Marnuk and the banits. He couldn't help Billy. The wise can't do anything to help anyone. His staff had no power against that creature because it was not under Voron's control. He looked again and again at his staff. Nothing. The beast was just a hunter, a creature that had to feed—nothing more.

But how can a leader leave his men, his friends? I didn't say anything about Shigash, a great warrior. That's because even I didn't know where he was. But now I can tell you that he was on the lake. He was on the lake's surface, with his legs in the water, but not deeper than his knees. He was sitting on something. The other two marnasits also were with him.

"Hamruk a thut!" he yelled in his language to them. "Hamruk a thut!"

And the marnasits hit the water again and again. And a blend of water and blood gushed every time when they hit the water. All the snakes began to scream. "It is true what Efreu said. It's only one creature. A creature with multiple heads."

Finally, after many cuts into the creature's body and in those snakes, the heads of the beast hid into the water. Billy was free now. Marnuk was swimming toward the others. One banit was also free, and Shigash and the marnasits were on the land now. In just few seconds the entire group was together, less one banit and the marnasit who was first caught.

All of them were running toward the woods. Who knew what else could attack them from the water? So it's better to leave the lake.

After they ran for more than three hundred meters, they stopped to take a breath. Efreu came near Shigash, who was covered with blood all over his body, and he said to him, "Once again you and your men saved us."

But the giant cut Efreu's words and said, "You very courage. This is most courage man," he said while he was looking at Billy. "We honored to fight for such warriors." Now he was looking to Emos. "Little but very good fighters. You almost lose life for Marnuk." What Shigash heard is 10 marnasits not kill creature like this. Nobody survived.

He looked to Efreu. He shook his hand and he continued, "But your courage . . . saved us."

And Shigash shook all the banits' hands. He began with Billy, Emos, and Hingus. Marnuk also touched the shoulders of these three brave men. He saluted the others. He owed his life to them.

"Only together we'll manage to kill any creature that might attack us. The marnasits warriors know well what kind of creatures we can meet. They have even fought with such creatures. And they defeated them."

"Words full of wise," Efreu said. He convinced the banits to listen to the marnasits' words even if they did not like to be led by those from the horde. The marnasits knew the dangers that existed on Mania or at least some of them, so they were those who came also led the group.

Everybody took a break to think. They thought about their lost friends. Good fighters. It's not right, probably they think. Too many friends were lost and will be lost. Those from the horde had almost vanished. The banits also lost those who remained to fight for Megros, and nobody was helping them. The evil forces were growing more and more. And there was nothing they can do about this.

"It's impossible to get through the woods to reach to Amnus," Emos broke the silence.

Even if the loss is painful, they had to go farther because they must protect those who were behind them.

"Yes, I know. We lost enough friends," said Efreu. "We must avoid these forests. Those who are coming after us must be protected. And these forests could hurt many of them. We must avoid the woods. But what else can we do?"

"We go to the lizard people," said Shigash. "They knew ways to reach Amnus."

"Are they dangerous?" asked Aarnos while he treated his wound.

"They are friends of us . . . or enemies, but until now they friends."

"I'm so relieved now," said Hingus ironically.

"We know lizards," said Shigash. "We made deal with them. They are hunters, like us. We agreed not fight between us. Enough prey for all of us. This means we shouldn't be concerned."

"Not exactly," said Emos, "because they may consider that we are their prey."

"They eat meat only . . . all kinds."

Efreu watched him with concern. He saw terrible things in these few days. After all this, you can expect anything from this planet.

All the group waited for an answer from Efreu. He was the one who should decide what they will do next. And the answer came, "We'll go to them. We don't have another option. If they are the friends of the horde, they could be ours too."

"Let's hope that they will remember that they are friends with these giants," said Hingus once again ironically.

The banits, including Aarnos, Emos, Hingus, and even Efreu, and the warriors from horde were afraid. Everyone wanted them dead. Besides the army of dead, in the woods were all sorts of animals, and now were those unknown lizards.

"Must leave . . . must keep going," said Shigash.

Then he made a sign to Marnuk.

"You go with Olaf. Tell lizards we approached. So nobody be hurt."

The two marnasits listened to what their leader had said. They began to run through those forests where the lizard men can be found.

"Only half a day to them. I know reach to them," said Shigash. "A safe way to them."

And the group followed the other two. They must go out from the woods, avoid the forests, and go among some giant rocks. These rocks could be also a threat for our heroes—and not only for them.

Soon Efreu and the others reunited with the large group. Those who reviewed their son, husband, or children were in high glee. Those who lost them, the parents of those two young banits who died, can only show their pain with lots of tears.

Those who still did not see their husband or son remained worried. In this case were two families. The families of two marnasits who Shigash sent to lizard men to announce their arrival.

The families of those who had died couldn't do anything more than cry.

"Welcome," said the elders to the small group. With them were also people from the horde. And they hugged, everyone with his family.

"Have you had problems in your way?" asked the elders.

"As you can see, some of us didn't return back to his family. Some creatures attacked us. Hardly had we escaped from the death's claws."

"We must stay away from water and forests. There are the most terrible creatures," said Shigash.

Some of the leaders looked not very friendly to those who were talking like Shigash.

"Listen to him," Emos tried to make them understand that Shigash is their friend. "He saved us many times from death. And we will do this many times from now on. Even if for this, he must give his life. That's why we must see him as a friend and show him respect."

"Who are you to tell us what should or shouldn't do?" said one of the elders. "You are a poor blacksmith. What do you know what is best for us? You have no right to—"

"He has no right to bid us, but he is right," said Efreu while he was approaching those who spoke. "You must treat them like our brothers. They are the only ones who know how to get rid of the creatures that live on this planet and that are so unknown for us."

"But they know only some of the creatures that live—"

"Yes, only some, my dear Mergoth, but you didn't even see those creatures," Efreu cut the elder's words. "You should know that what you have heard from the ancestor's stories we saw and we fight with. And you also should know that it's much worse than you heard in stories."

"Most go Amnus . . . quick," said Shigash to those from the elders.

"We'll go then," said Efreu. "The same group."

"No!" said Shigash to him with the same clumsy words he used in speaking. "Too many. Only some of us go. Lizard men afraid if too many. They attack and kill us."

"Emos, Billy, Hingus, be ready. You'll come with me and Shigash. The rest of you stay with our brothers and sisters," said the old man to the other banits. "We'll meet Marnuk and Olaf when we reach to those lizard men."

"How can you have so much trust into them?" said one voice from the elders.

"Yes, don't trust them."

"Maybe they and the lizards work together on something. Maybe they want to kill you, another one."

"Enough!" yelled Efreu. "They saved our lives. And they did this more than once. So don't dare to accuse them about anything.

We lost enough time with such discussions. I said that we can trust them, and we should keep going if we want to save our lives."

The elders dissipated into the crowd. It's obvious that they didn't want to obey Efreu's words, but there was nothing they can do. Efreu helped the banits so many times. So they can't hurt him—at least, not now. Maybe later, after he will do some mistakes; maybe after that, people won't obey him.

"We should go now," said Efreu to his group. Only those who heard their names headed for the gate.

"And that little boy," said Shigash.

A moment of silence. Nobody said anything for five seconds. Efreu stopped. He turned around and saw who that little boy was. But why should he go with them? What was the need for him?

"This won't happen. He's just a kid," the one who spoke strongly was Billy.

"But I could carry Hingus's spears," said Rahnab, Billy's brother.

"You have no right to speak!" he yelled to the little boy while he was throwing a cutting look at him. After that, he continued a little bit more calmly, "This is not your concern," said Billy to his brother.

"But I think he's right. I could use him to carry my spears." Hingus smiled to Billy.

Giant Billy said nothing this time. He just looked to Hingus with such anger that even the proud man understood that he shouldn't joke about that.

"You still don't know what a joke is," said Hingus. "All of us know that this child should not come with us, right?"

Hingus tried to repair his mistake. He looked at Efreu while he said that Rahnab shouldn't go with them and wait for the wise man's approval.

Efreu sighed and then, with sorrow in his heart, said, "Warrior Shigash helped us many times. His ideas were always full of success. And all of you saw that. I just hope that he'll be right this time too. But let's hope that God is also with us. So let's go then."

"But, wise man—" Billy tried to interfere.

"Our future is more important than anything. So we'll bring your brother with us," said Efreu to Billy.

Then the old man bowed his head, and he continued with sadness, "And God will help us. He always takes care of those who really need Him, especially when those are only defenseless children, like Rahnab is."

After he said these words Efreu left his friends to speak with the elders.

"But he's just a child," said Billy to those who remained there. He looked at Emos and even to Hingus but with fear this time. "He's just a child," he said while he was looking around. He was searching for some help from one of his friends. But none of them can help you. None of them had the courage to confront Efreu's words. So the group began to break up, and everyone went to his family. Even Rahnab went to his parents and happily told them that he will go with Billy, Efreu, and the others. Such an honor for him. But his parents were also sad, and they were crying. They knew about the danger.

All of them went to their families, except Billy and Shigash. Billy's face was filled with hatred and thirst for revenge. From now on, for him the marnasit was the one who killed his little brother because his brother was good as dead. But there was a little hope because Billy would rather give his life than let his brother to die.

But only if he could to protect the little one because everywhere they went there was only danger, and Rahnab had almost no chance in this wilderness. How could a child escape before a danger like a csillias is or before a hynd? Many warriors like that marnasit died because of that creature. Good warriors like those banits—how could a child escape?

While he was thinking at these, he met Shigash's eyes. The giant looked at him with sadness. It looked like Shigash was regretting that he had to do such a thing—that is, take Rahnab with them.

But Billy didn't care about that.

"I will take care of you. I promise that," said giant Billy while he looked at Shigash with hate.

The giant looked down. He knew why he took the boy with them. He was the only one who knew why. Later, maybe all of them will find out too. None of the others knew, but they figured that it had to be a serious reason because you can't take a child to death. You can't!

But whatever the reason was, Shigash also hadn't enough trust about the decision he made. From his look, you can figure that he had some trail of uncertainty. He didn't let that be seen by others. In these hard times he can't do anything else. And he was the only one who knew what they were going to face into their journey.

"We are ready to go!" you can hear Efreu's words. And all those who take part of that group began to move including Efreu, Emos, Shigash, Hingus, Rahnab, and even Billy. The other marnasit also remained with the group. His strength and his experience as a warrior will help the group; they needed him.

"Take care of yourselves. Be careful!" you can hear from the their relatives between cries and tears.

"Let's hope that God will hear our prayers, and we'll meet again!" some voices said.

And all the heroes disappeared between the rocks.

"Hingus, can I use a spear of yours if I have to fight with monsters?" asked Rahnab with full enthusiasm.

"Certainly," replied Hingus. And he gave a spear to Rahnab.

The one who was prouder than anyone and never gave anything to anyone was now a different person. He looked at the boy with compassion and mercy. However, he was only a boy. And Hingus asked himself, "Why must a child see such terrible events? Why did the Creator put this innocent child in such difficulties?"

But the boy was so happy that he will fight against enemies.

"I can't wait to fight with them," said the boy while he was trying to use the spear as best as he can. But he only hurt him easily with the spear.

"Only if he knows what we have to face with. But he mustn't know. Not until we have to face them," Hingus thought.

"And besides any of my spears, you can base on my arm." Hingus smiled at Rahnab. "Together we'll kill any monsters that dare to disturb us."

When he heard that Hingus will take care of him, the boy became more excited. He considered Hingus as an example to follow. And he knew that the great warrior Hingus was going to take care of him better than anyone.

"We'll kill these beasts!" yelled the child. "Nothing can stop us."

Billy, who was near them, listened to their talk. He was less sad now because Hingus looked like he was a great man, after all. And he was going to take care of his brother too. All of them will. He was certain by that!

But why must his brother face so heavy testing? He was so angry. Angry because of Shigash. Every time Shigash said something about the way they had to follow, Billy showed his dissatisfaction. If they had to go near a cluster of trees or a very small lake, he looked unsatisfied by the marnasit's choice.

"Why not we go on that bridge? If it was built, it means that those who built it did that to get over it."

"Lizard-people built bridge to feed creature same blood as they. Their blood is not like mine or you. Cold blood. Like reptiles," responded Shigash. "Snake, furnus, and even hynd are in lake . . . lizard-people friends. I sure if they had chosen between me, you and snakes, they don't choose me and you. But you do same with enemies." Shigash looked at Billy and then at Rahnab.

"What a furnus is?" asked Rahnab while he was listening their conversation. After he played a while as a hunter, after he looked in every bush for the monsters, he got bored. He moved his attention to Shigash. This was a mountain for him. "So tall and so strong is the giant," he said. "But Hingus could take him down easily."

"Horrible bird . . . great theet," said Shigash.

Furnus were like some birds, but instead of a beak they had a mouth like the banits, and they also had some teeth like predators. In fact, they were predators. They were carnivores. Like lizard people, they ate any meat. Theirs legs had stong claws like the eagle's; with them the furnus could raise even three banits in the air at the same time. Their bodies were not very large. They were about the size of a marnasit, also having a power as great as theirs.

Besides being a good warrior, Shigash was also wise. His wisdom came from his travels. From his experiences.

But even so, Billy couldn't suffer the giant at all because the marnasit had taken the decision to take his brother in this hard journey. Even the gesture was a noble one, even if to save the others, any sacrifice must be done. Billy can't understand why it has to be sacrified immolated. He was just a kid. He could not understand it. He did not want to understand this. So he could only hate Shigash.

Passing through many canyons, places where water and life entirely was missing and where you can see only sands, passing through places where you can see only very high and steep cliffs, which there is no way to get on, passing through places where you can see ruins, which were remained from some unknown ancient civilizations, after two days of speed travel through desert, Shigash finally stopped in front of a forest which came up from nowhere and said to the others.

"We arrived theirs territory. Be careful," he whispered to his companions. "They near."

This area where their territory began had started with this forest—a dense forest. There were no trees such as an imensialiss type, but there also were large trees. Their crown began to grow near the ground. A marnasit couldn't cross beneath them without bending; even a banit will touch the crown of the tree with a top of the head if he didn't bow a little bit. Near these trees were some high and dense herbs and bushes. Scarcely could you pass through this forest. Our travelers made their way through the bushes by cutting them with their swords, breaking them with their hand, using their legs to put them to the ground. But even so it was very hard to penetrate this green wall.

"Won't tormented us for long," said Shigash to the others. Tree wall thin. After we cross wall, we find easy route to cross."

"I can't wait to let behind these 'tools of torture.' I can't wait to get rid of the pain caused by these bushes," said Rahnab, the child.

This time the one who encouraged the boy was Shigash, the giant who treated everyone with usual hardness, now he showed his gentleness. The marnasit put gently his hand on the boy's shoulder and said to him, "Soon we get off green curtain . . . will be much easy to you."

The boy breathed a sigh of relief. And he continued to cross through the bushes.

Indeed not after a long time, they finally crossed the thin wall.

"Now we must be very careful. Don't let them to see us first," said Billy to the group.

"They saw us," replied Shigash. "But be careful. Lizard people make many mistakes. They say that not purpose. They say that because they not see well, but they see better then all of us. Not just once killed someone because their thirst for blood."

"It means they are like those from the legion of the dead," whispered Hingus.

"Not really. Unlike those form the legion, the lizard people ponder the facts first and only then go for it. It's true they had some moments when they get some radical measures without knowing the exact situation, but they usually think about before they do anything. Of course, they take the decision, which is best for them, but let's hope the best for them is to fight with us against evil. We need their help. Those from the legion of the dead will destroy everything in their path without any thinking. They will do anything their master Voron wants. He thinks for them and tells them what to do. And nowhere in his thoughts is a room for those who are faithful to the Creator. That's us, and any life creature, even the lizard people. Let's hope that they understood that."

All those words came from Efreu. In the last two days, Efreu said almost nothing to the others. He didn't speak. When somebody asked him something, he answered with a sign of yes or no. Nothing more.

But now he spoke like he knew the lizards even if he and the other banits never traveled far from their castle's walls. But the truth is that nobody really knew how and when this prophet Efreu appeared in their lives.

"Something is happening there at that cluster of those small trees," interrupted Emos.

Emos, very cautious at every time, saw some movement there while Efreu was speaking to the group. He listened to Efreu's words like the others, but he also watched so nobody will be hurt.

Everybody looked in that direction. And they were surely saved by God. Almost at the same time they had looked there, two arrows came very fast toward them and almost hit Shigash and Hingus. But the marnasit and the banit managed to avoid the arrows.

"See, this I say to you. Although we sent our friends to lizard people, lizards attacked us. They tried to scare us. If want to kill some they could easily."

Not so far, you can see the lizard men's camp. One of the lizard people had made a sign to the others to let the bows down. He smiled. This meant that what Shigash said was true. The lizards knew that the marnasits and "the others" would come. I mean "the others" because the banits never saw such creatures like the lizards; perhaps even the lizards also hadn't met any banit. Unlike the other lizard men, this lizard was dressed with simple cloths, and he had some hat on his head. The others were wearing only some kind of pants, made from some kind of barks.

These lizard men were some . . . lizards. The only difference between them and other lizards was that these lizard men were standing in two legs. They were almost as big as the marnasits, but they were thinner than them. Their head was like a lizard's head, more like the chameleon's head. Their eyes were looking everywhere—at everyone. Their skin was also like the chameleon's.

Maybe they can also change the color of their skin, but I'm not sure yet. I've never seen any of these chameleons changing their skin into the environment's color and hiding.

After that the lizard men's leader made a sign to others to move toward our heroes.

When between the two groups was only a short distance, the lizard leader said, "Friend Sshigassh, long time, no ssee. What honor brought you to usss?"

"Perhaps my friend I sent to you told what want. Hope he still alive," said the giant Shigash.

"Maybe he iss. Maybe he iss not. Depend of what news you bring to uss."

For our group of heroes and for every one of us, these words meant that Efreu and the others must be most careful with these creatures. Billy, Hingus, and Emos prepared their weapons to fight against these creatures. The lizard-archers prepared theirs bows. The lizard leader saw that the banits understood that the problem was more delicate. They understood that these lizards didn't want at all to make a partnership with the banits and the marnasits.

But Shigash was so calm. He knew something that the others didn't know.

"We brought the niptus!" he said. And he said these words so loud that everybody heard him. Everyone was scared when they heard these words. All the lizard men were scared. Even the leader. Even some lizards that remained in camp stood up when they heard these words. They were also scared. Even the banits who didn't know anything about this niptus were very scared. Actually they were more scared than anyone. They were scared because they never met such creatures like these lizard men, creatures more terrifying than the marnasits. And they also didn't know what a niptus was and how he can help them.

Even if the lizard men were more scared than ever, they didn't show the fear on their faces. Maybe it's because they were trained to keep their temper, or their faces can't show any gesture. Which lizard can do this? But one proof of terror can be their silence.

After a small break, the leader finally said something, "Although we knew that this day will come, how do we know that this day has arrived warrior, Shigash?"

He must be strong for his men.

But this time Reptoc spoke with more respect with Shigash than the first time. He knew that whatever Shigash said may be true. Shigash never spoke about something unless he knew that he was almost sure. Maybe the giant hoped that if he'll help Rahnab, they will succeed. Or maybe he really thought that the child was niptus. Maybe he saw a sign. Maybe he knew something from his ancestors. Or maybe . . . maybe he was just hoping so because they had no other hope than this one. They must survive as long as they can. They needed help from someone. But now, their only hope was Rahnab, the niptus.

"I know this is niptus. He traveled with us. Give us proof of courage. Fought against very dangerous creatures. Even survived battle with a hynd while others not survived. Good fighters not survived," said the giant Shigash with breaks. But even if he spoke hardly, with pretty long breaks so he can find his words, nobody disturbed him. Every word was listened by everyone: banits, lizard men, and marnasits.

The banits were also scared, almost more scared than the lizards. They were scared because they knew that not every word from the little story Shigash said was true. They also didn't know anything of what the leader and Shigash were speaking. What was this niptus that brought so much terror on the entire group of lizards?

Suddenly Reptoc began to look to everyone. He looked at Emos, Hingus, and the others.

All eyes were looking at the boy. And all these warriors, all the lizard men, were now more scared than probably they've ever been. From their ancestors, the lizard men knew that when the niptus will come, the end of their world is near.

The boy, Rahnab, was also a little scared, but he tried not to let anyone see that.

Emos, Hingus, and even Aarnos saw that Shigash and the lizard people spoke about the child as a character who is going to fulfill a prophecy, a prophecy that only Shigash and the reptiles knew.

The lizards had a tremendous stature. They were as huge as Shigash, also with an incredible power. Their skin had the color of the environment in which they were at that moment. They could be green; they could be black or almost any other color. They could be white maybe. Who knows?

And all these because they were like chameleons that we knew. They were taller than the banits but had a similar body. These creatures were bipedal, had two hands, two legs, like banits, but they had a tail. The head was also as same as the banit's head, but they didn't have lips. They had a small mouth that ended with some kind of a very short beak. On top of their head was an extension of the skull. This extension of the skull was easily visible to older ones. The youth had a sort of horn in the forehead, which will turn into a shield for the head when they will reach an older age. You can see that in the elders.

But the most interesting thing was that they could look with an eye in one direction and the other in another direction as a chameleon. So they could see everything around them, with a 360-degree view. This and the power made them, as probably we will see, the best archers on Mania.

"Come talk to our leader," said Reptoc with the same calm that he tried hardly to display all this time.

"Come," said Shigash.

So the heroes and the lizard people were pointing to some very high rocks, which nearly seemed to touch the sky. The group was in the middle while the lizard people went ahead and behind them. The heroes were kept as prisoners.

"We will go on Vale of Tears. Ketos, our master, is there. The Vale of Tears is on that mountain that you can see from here," said Reptoc, pointing in that direction. It was a huge mountain.

"Also there is our Queen of Sheba," added Reptoc.

When he pronounced the name of the queen, Reptoc looked very carefully at Shigash. The marnasit tried one's hardest not to draw any gesture of fear, and he succeeded. He continued to walk unaffected at all.

Seeing the news that his queen and leader were in the same place did not affect Shigash, Reptoc showed much concern about it. But even so he tried to walk like a leader to show to his men that they had nothing to fear about.

"Rahnab, me tell you this," whispered Shigash to Billy's brother. "All should hear this. Come near," he said while he looked around to make sure that the lizard didn't hear their discussion.

But the lizards kept a safe distance. Reptoc and the lizards had their secrets and discussions. So they were those who wanted to stay away as much as they can.

Seeing that, Shigash continued, "Rahnab, must save us. You're niptus. Niptus is savior. For we . . . for they niptus is bad prophet. He kill the queen. Queen die, end of them. Queen lives, they dominate. So they want and not want the niptus. Cruel queen, bloodthirsty queen, a queen fed with fresh meat. She and her maids fed by lizard. Niptus they do not want, they no want savior. They enjoy their life. They like hunt almost all living beings, for their queen, maids of queen and for them. They do everything fight against you. Stop you kill queen."

"Let him save us? Let him kill the queen?" asked the very nervous Billy. "He must kill the queen? Do it yourself!" While he was yelling at Shigash, Billy pushed the giant with such strength that Shigash almost fell down. And perhaps if the others weren't there, Billy would start a fight. Each one, Emos and Hingus, took one of Billy's arms, but even so they barely could keep Billy.

"Me can't kill queen. He only . . . has right approach creature."

"I knew . . . I knew we cannot trust you," said Billy while he was trying again to reach and punch the marnasit.

But everything calmed down when Efreu came and said, "We must trust each other."

Everybody looked now at Efreu.

Efreu took a look to the lizard people. The lizards saw the fight between banits and marnasits, but they didn't intervene. Even if our heroes would kill each other, the reptiles would only watch the slaughter. They would be happy if they see blood—they wanted to see blood.

Also they weren't afraid by the coming of the niptus, like many of us who aren't afraid by God's judging. That child, Rahnab, couldn't kill a mysterious creature like their queen. Any of them could kill the boy in one second. So their queen will do that in less time.

So the lizards weren't so panicked. They were only bored, and this old man only destroyed a moment of fun for them.

"We must trust each other," intervened Efreu. "All of us want to save our family, especially our children. But none of you should punish Shigash for what he had done. Perhaps this was the only way to intervene in the lives of these creatures, creatures that we could not avoid because we had to contact them in our way because we need three keys to open Amnus gates. And one of these keys is on the queen's throat."

The group was very surprised to hear that. It was clearly visible on their faces that they were concerned about it like it wasn't enough that Amnus was n so far away and the road was so full of danger. Now they had to find those keys to open the gate, or else everything will be in vain.

This time, Emos couldn't stay calm.

"Wise Efreu," said Emos, "why don't you tell us about these things? I think it was our right to know these. It is our right and those who come behind us. We must know what we have to face."

Emos was very nervous. He felt that he was betrayed by the one he considered his father and best advisor.

The old man looked at Emos, then at the others. Fear and despair could be read on their faces. If wise Efreu would fail in convincing our heroes that they must fight, then there is a chance to fight against Voron, Lord of darkness, then everything was lost. All those who came behind them—women, old men, and children—all were lost. Everything depended on the success of these heroes. But now their success seemed to be more far than ever—at least in their view.

But they were right to lose courage. As prisoners of those lizard people, disappointed and somehow betrayed by the person who led them, they could die by Voron's sword. If this would happen, they would become forever soldiers of Voron; they would become some bloodthirsty soldiers, soldiers that surely would kill other innocents as they were at this moment.

And so the army of Voron would increase more and more and would become indestructible.

Even Shigash lost his courage. You can see that in his eyes. Almost all his people were destroyed. Only some of them escaped. He always was the one that told everyone they should fight against the shadow army because they will win. But now almost everything seemed to be lost. Mankind, the marnasits and the banits, seemed to be lost forever.

After another few hours of walked, the group consisted of banits, marnasits, and lizard men finally reached those far rocks. There was a camp with dozen of reptiles.

Once they had got closer to a tent, Reptoc talked, "There is the tent where you will stay until the next morning. It is too dangerous for us to go now because of predatory birds that hunt in the night. You'll get something to eat and some water to drink to show our hospitality, and then you can rest."

After that, Reptoc gave some indications to his soldiers.

Hearing the noise from the tent, the two marnasits came out. Everybody was happy to review them, even the banits. But it was a bitter joy on their faces.

Some of our heroes sat near a fire. Billy was staying somewhere in the dark. He was thinking on something. Efreu also was staying alone. He meditated, or he was praying.

Acttualy all of them thought at something. Even they stayed togheter; they didn't speak to each other. You can see on their faces that as more time passed and the more they thought about what they had to face, the more disappointed and desperate they were. Their courage and the will to do everything to help those who came behind them were not as intense as before. None of them no longer had the same desire to fight against evil because their confidence that they will win in this battle was destroyed. It seemed like when everything was working better and they can hope that they will succeed, another very hard obstacle appeared, an obstacle that could not be avoided and against whom they could not fight.

Efreu saw all of them destroyed because of the news they received. He sighed, and he said, "Can you imagine what effect it would have if I said these things to the whole crowd? More of them would stay in the city from the shore of Megros. The despair would have stopped us all in that city. And most of us would have died. Maybe all of us because everyone who stayed there we all know what had happened," Efrau said with pain in his heart.

The group listened to him more and more carefully. Efreu was the only one who can raise up their spirits. The two tribes depended on the heroes' help—on their success. And surely they did not really know what hardships came behind them. Maybe everything really would have happened like Efreu said. All would have died. Maybe it was better that only they knew the truth.

"Efreu is also right this time," said Emos with less conviction than usual. "They do not need to know what awaits us," he continued.

"He right," Shigash said. "Enough we only know. News destroy last hope spark. Gate only way to escape eternal death."

Bily, Hingus, and two others were not quite so benevolent. They could not understand why everything had to be more and more difficult. And besides that, even Efreu made everything more difficult.

"Even we find early about heavy events still can not do something," continued Shigash. „No chance for we. Maybe we still not have any, but we must try. If not for we, then for our fathers, mothers, brothers, and sisters. For families and friends. Everything depends on us."

"He is right. The succes of our tribes depends on us. We must not to get into the hands of our enemies, so we can have an eternal life beside our creator."

"And we all know that if we get into the hands of Lord of Darkness, we will have to be his servants in all the wars he will take to destroy everything that was created by the Creator," said Emos.

It looks like Emos can't be angry at Efreu.

"Now you can see why I didn't announce it to you earlier," said Efreu. „You are the only ones who can make these days full of pain to become full of joy and peace. You were chosen for this because if you can safely pass all these tests, then there is none that can do it. Only you can help me save the banits and the marnasits from slavery."

"And we'll help you with that," intervened Rahnab. Although he was the youngest and the most inexperienced, he seemed to understand that Efreu just wanted to see his people saved.

Finally our heroes began to understand Efreu's facts. At least some of them. However, it seemed that Efreu really took wise decisions in all aspects. Every choice was taken only after long thoughts.

"Maybe it's true what you say," adressed Billy to Efreu. "But I'm tired of so many secrets. First I hear that my brother must fight against a creature about which we know nothing, not even how it looks like, and then I find out that everything we do, all the sacrifices we made and those we will make, all these could be in vain."

"It's true," intervened Hingus. "We do not know anything about that queen and her maids. From what I understood from Shigash, it seems that the lizard people are against us. In fact, definitely they are against us. How can we fight against them?"

"It will be very difficult, but what else we can do?" Efreu said again. "We're the only who can resist them because we must and because God said so and He will help us."

"Me know if someone will save us from hand of darkness, only him," said a voice from the marnasits. But this wasn't Shigash. Marnuk was the one who spoke while he looked at Efreu because he spoke about him.

The banits asked themselves why the marnasit had so much confidence in Efreu. He only knew him for a few days.

They were even more surprised when they heard Shigash's words, "Marnuk speak true. Only wise Efreu can help us got out this mess. So said my elders. They said will come day when we must deal difficult moments. And who speak with angels will be helped by God and save us. This is the prophecy."

Who was this Efreu? Where did he come from? None of the banits had ever asked themselves where Efreu came.

But now they are asking.

"Me, you and the others, we all know that we Efreu was announced many times about the dangers that were coming upon Megrosului, about the drought that came five years ago, about the fire that could destroy more than half of Megros if Efreu wouldn't say to us that a fire storm will come upon us. Who knows how many people could die if we weren't warned by him? He also said that Megos will be destryed, but our brothers didn't listen him," he spoke those last words with sadness in his heart.

"And now they are last."

"I am sory that I couldn't convince them to come with us. But this was the Lord's will. I see only what the Creator wants me to see. And I succeed only in what God wants to succeed. And every decision I take is the Most High's desires. Even if I do not discuss with Him, even if I don't hear His voice, I speak to his servants."

"We know, Great Efreu," Emos spoke again. „And we're sorry that we doubted about the choices you've made. You choose to hide certain things and to show us just what our minds can understand, for our own good. And with that, you gave hope to our people. From now on, we will not doubt about any decision you take, isn't so, Bily?"

Emos looked at his friend.

"Yes, we'll never doubt about what Efreu will choose," replied the giant but slowly and with so little hope in his voice.

After a short time, while none of the others said anything because all of them knew that Billy was sadder than ever, the giant continued, "But all of you must understand that I am worried about my brothers and my relatives. First of all for Rahnab because he must be with us and he must bear the brunt of this mission, like we all do. I'm worried for him, and because of that, I easily lose confidence in everything."

And looking toward Efreu, he bowed his head ashamed and said, "I apologize for my behavior and my words."

"I also apologize for everything, and I think all of us feel the same," Emos spoke again. "If even the marnasits have so much confidence in you, then we also should have more confidence in you. And we must understand that even if everything is going to be harder, Great Efreu would have done everything in his power. Therefore, we must help him because the success also depends on us. We could grab a good decision and do like Wise Efreu is asking us, or we could not listen him, and then I'm sure we will lose everything. We will lose ourselves and those whom we love."

"Wise words you spoke," Efrau said, smiling slightly.

"Indeed. Seems young banit is not only good warrior, also very wise," said Shigash, looking at the others. "He great leader," he continued.

Then the marnasit's leader said to Billy, "Everything wise said is true. Difficult times elders talked about now happened. And only wise Efreu understand language Lord of Light and servants of him spoke. So must believe he is prophet. He only speak that language."

Marnuk intervened again, "Now our concern is help this poor child kill the beast queen, like lizard prophecy said. Us must make plan kill the creature." He spoke slow and hard like Shigash did. Actually any marnasit spoke the same way.

"Let's get inside the tent," said Efreu. „There we can speak without being spied by these lizard men."

Everyone stood up and headed through that big tent. Even Bily stood up from the tree trunk. And finally he entered into the tent. He knew that they must work together if they wanted to have any chance to escape from this danger. But it's hard for him and also for the others. He can't forget how some of his friends had been killed by those creatures, and none could do anything to save them from death. Also none of them, even Efreu, was able to convince those people to leave the city of Megros because they couldn't face that army. And all of them had perished.

Besides all these, his brother should fight with them to get out from this lizard's trouble. A child. So it's clear that Billy can't have the same confidence as he once had.

Shigash extinguished the fire in front of the tent with some water, and then he entered into the tent. They all needed to discuss, but he left the impression that they wanted to sleep. That's because even though it was not so obvious, some of the lizard people were "watching." And our heroes knew that. But they didn't show it. They behaved normally.

They also knew that the lizard's leader and some of his men climbed the rocky hill, which was in front of them, and something was happening. Probably they will announce to the king about niptus. Or to their queen. Or they will make some plans to kill our group of heroes.

"Have you seen how many guys have left?" asked Hingus when entering the tent.

"They were more than thirty, and they looked carefully at the sky like something could attack them at any moment. It means that we have not lied about those eagles," answered Emos.

Efreu made some light with his scepter inside the tent. The others drew on their faces a little smile.

Rahnab said, smiling more than all the others, "You can make light where is dark. It means that our Lord is with you . . . with us."

If Efreu couldn't use his sceptre, which none knew where it came from, before, now he can use it when he needed it. But he was not as happy as the others. He said, "This is not a happy moment. If my scepter is more and more powerful, it means that the obstacles we have to face are more and more difficult."

He adjusted the light from his scepter because he didn't want to bring the lizards' attention. They also whispered to one another when someone had something to say. And two or three banits were watching those who will enter the tent. Every time they saw someone was approaching, they made a signal, and all of them kept silent. When the danger had passed, they continued their discussion.

Two lizard archers entered inside the roomy tent. Inside. On the ground were some skins of animals hunted by these predators. Looking at these furs, you can see they were skilled hunters. If not better than the marnasits, then at least as good as them. There were some furs which not even Shigash could say Shigash whose fierce animals belong. Some of them were so big that all the group cuold sleep on it.

Raptoc joined inside. Reptoc spoke, addressing and looking only at the marnasits. For them only the marnasits were great warriors—dangerous opponents. The others, the banits, the lizards didn't ever hear something about them. And such little creatures can't be opponents for such great hunters like they were. At least so the lizard men believed about Efreu and the banits.

"Brother Sshigassh," he said in a false friendly manner to the warrior, "lasst night I had the courasse and recklessnesss to go to my master. We talk about thiss niptusss. If thiss creature, which doess not sseem very frightening, is the one that should ssave us from 'sslavery,' to which we are exposed by our queen, then I think you should talk with our king."

Then he approached Shigash and told him, "If one of you iss going to kill the niptus and ssave uss from the pain of losing our queen, we'll let you out of here safely and unharmed."

"Us can't kill. You can't kill. Nobody can," said Shigash aloud, so everyone could hear him.

When he heard these words, Reptoc became angry.

Bily became worried. He stood up and caught the axe ready anytime to protect his brother. The others also were ready anytime to fight for Rahnab's life.

One of the two archers immediately touched him with the head of an arrow on his throat with one eye staring at Billy and with the other one staring at the others. He also made some noise with his split tongue like snakes do. Immediately a few archers entered into the tent, and they were looking with their eyes everywhere, staring into one person, with his arrow pointing into that direction, and looking to another potential victim.

Shigash made a sign to his friends to let down their arms. But only when they saw that Efreu also made a sign did they leave their weapons. Reptoc approached Bily and put a some kind of knife to his neck as . . . rather a beast's fang. He made a sign to his people to take all the weapons in possession of our heroes. All the weapons were taken.

"You have no chance." Reptoc smile again, a sort of bloodthirsty smile.

"But prophecy forbid kill us. Only queen can. Else, Lord of Light punish all you."

Reptoc's smile immediately faded. The reptile headed toward Shigash and said with disdain, "Too bad we could have a good alliance together. We still can have if you kill thesse half manesssi."

"Manessi" meant "coward" for the reptiles. Half of "manessi" was a bigger insult.

"They proved were not manessi. They brave. Us don't kill them. Let queen try."

"Sshe will ssucceed," said Reptoc again. "You have no weaponss. Our prophecy ssaid that the niptusss should kill our queen with hiss bare handss."

"Not true," answered Shigash.

"Yess, I know. You caught me. It doesn't say that. But it also doesn't say that I should give him weapons." And he smiled again.

This time his smile had a strong effect even on Shigash. Their queen could not be less stronger than them. Their queen was perhaps a little larger than them—or at least he hoped so. Certainly they must kill the queen and take from her neck what was one of the keys from the gate of Amnus unarmed or at least untill they'll find some weapons.

Reptoc bothered the warrior again. "Prepare yourself for traveling. A nice trip . . . I hope," and he smiled again. "You should know there is a possibility that this niptus won't arrive to meet our queen. If you will arrive safely. But you shouldn't be worried. We'll take care of you."

After saying these words while all the time smiling, the izard man got out of the tent. When out, he gave orders to five of his men to guard the tent.

"Without weapons, we are lost," said Bily to the others.

"But we still have each other. We must take care of us, especially the litlle one," said Efreu.

"Especially him," completed Shigash. "Without him, we lost."

"I have these two knives," said Rahnab.

The boy took those two knives and gave them to Shigash. Nobody had searched the boy. The truth is that nobody expected this child to have weapons. It was too feeble and too weak in their eyes—couldn't be dangerous for them. They could kill him in just a second. But they could not do so because the prophecy said that if "niptus" did not fight with the queen because of problems that arose because of them, their people will be buried forever in the Pit of the Lost. This prophecy scared the lizard people.

"See . . . real niptus. Already helped us."

He took the two knives and gave one to Emos and one to Hingus.

"Us can fight bare hands against lizard." And he was right. Those from the horde and Billy were so strong that they can fight against the lizards with their bare hands. But Emos and Hingus were good fighters with weapons.

"It might be true what Reptoc said. Maybe these rocks hide some dangers. So we must take care."

But Hingus didn't finish his words. From outside, the reptile's voice was heard again, "Let'ss go!"

Some guards entered the tent and invited the heroes out.

When our group got outside, they saw the preparation for a long journey. Some lizard people gathered and packed the tents. Others put the luggage on some beasts, some reptiles bigger than them and marnasits. The marnasits had never seen some of these beasts, but the banits never seen any of these. Some of them were more little than the others, but few of them were enormous. The banits were amazed by how some little creatures like these lizards, little in comparison with those incredible beasts, could domesticate such beasts. The banits were amazed, but they were also scared because those beasts were very nervous. One or two creatures didn't stay calm. They were moving all around. And one of those two was gigantic. Probably the bigest creature from Mania. It was moving her enormous body and tail. When the beast moved it and hit one of the archer lizard, the lizard was thrown onto a tree with such power that he couldn't stand up alone. Reptoc made a sign to the other two. They took him, put him on some luggage and tied him up on them, like it was some garbage.

Reptoc approached our group and said, "We'll get on that path up through the mountain," he said to Shigash.

It was a fairly narrow path, which climbed on the mountain outside busy. It is very much to walk until destination and the road seemed very tedious and full of dangers, because they were always exposed.

"Let'ss go!" said Reptoc when he saw that everything was tight and his men were ready to go.

The journey begun. The marnasits and the banits were somewhere between the lizards. Perhaps they were held in the middle for better supervision. But maybe it was better for them that way. They were safer in that way. Or maybe not.

They were walking for several hours on that path, which was leading to the mountaintop. This mountain was so tall that it looked like it was touching the sky. Probably it would have taken several days to reach on top of that mountain. This mountain's name was Vorniht Gassar. It meant "bridge between the Creator and people" in the ancestors' language.

They say that if you climb this mountain and get on top of it, you'll reach the gate of the city where Gabriel, Michael, and other bands of angels who serve the Creator lived once. A place where the first ancestors of banits and marnasits, because they have the same ancestors, also lived. But now, their ancestors are gone, and the angels went somewhere else.

It was a mountain that you can see from everywhere you looked; it was that high. But this was not just a high mountain. It was a very stretched mountain. And everywhere there were smaller peaks, which hid many dangers behind them. All the mountain looked like a huge maze, if you looked from the sky. A maze with of unequal walls, a labyrinth full of dangers, a maze with many unknown paths. Some of the paths led you to destination; others led you to the shortest way: death. If you do not know the exact path, you can lose your way, or you could not ever get out of this maze.

"Many have perisshed here. Many of thesse roads lead to mountaintop, other roadss at itsss foot. But if you do not know the way, you can get to a point in front of a huge rock wall, and then you have to go back in your way. But alsso you cannot find the ssame road, which will lead to your doom, and thosse who have accompanied you. Many of our brothersss were losst. We found their bodiess. We alsso found through our journeyss boness from many large creaturesss, dangerouss creaturess, ssome of them with wingsss. Sso if thosse creaturess with wingss couldn't essscape from thesse placess, ssurely you can't," said Reptoc.

As an argument against his words, they all heard a strong and fierce rage. It was clear that behind the wall of their left was one of those dangerous creatures. It probably smelled them. Luckily there was a wall between them.

"And I'm ssure that there iss ssomething in thisss mountain pathss, deadly creaturess, sso be careful which path you'll take when you'll return," completed Reptoc.

Even if they will succeed to get out safely from their meeting with that queen, our heroes still had a problem: how to return to theirs families.

The banits, hearing these words, became more cautious of the way, so they can observe things that could help them on return. But because of the very high and straight walls and because of the narrow paths, you couldn't get a lot of guidance points. Almost everything was the same. Rocks, rocks, and rocks. No tree. Like they went through the same place several times.

"Trust our Lord," told Efreu from time to time to increase their courage.

"We'll find a way to return. But now we must focus on the fight with lizard queen."

However they tried to resolve the situation, they couldn't do that. So I think their morale was low. And there was not much you can do to raise their morale, perhaps because their faith was not so strong. Perhaps it's because they couldn't belive that the Creator will help them. Or maybe it was hard to believe in their own strengths. Only the Lord of Light knew how everything was going to happen.

Suddenly the lizard people became agitated. And they had a reason. If you looked up, you could see how some creatures fly above the heads of the advancing group members. You could not see them for long because the road was narrow, the walls of the labyrinth were very high, and the winged creatures disappeared very quickly. But you can see clearly that the winged creatures were observing our heroes and their companions.

The lizards were very scared because of those creatures. It's sure that they had met the winged beasts in the past.

"Sit down if you want to remain alive," said Reptoc but not to Efreu or to the others. The message was for his fellows. Certainly Reptoc didn't care what would happen to those they were guarding.

The lizards prepared their arrows and bows. One of them had wanted to shoot those flying creatures that flew around them, but Reptoc stopped him.

"Don't shoot. Our arrows would only make them more aggressive," whispered the lizard leader to his men.

At some point, the group reached a place where the walls were far and the opening to the sky was higher. One of those winged came down slightly toward the group and landed on a rock. There were some large stones, and on one of them the bird landed. In fact, it was not a bird; it was rather an animal with wings and covered with feathers only on his wings. The rest of its body was covered with fur. It had a bird head indeed, with a strong beak, but it had feet. It looked almost like a lion but with a bird head. It was standing on its back feet like a banit, but surely it could stay like a lion on all four feet. He was a creature named Ianus, a creature that looked like half lion and half eagle, but it was huge. His arms were like a lion's arms and his feet like an eagle's claws. And it had a tail like a lion's tail. A strange creature.

The Ianus watched quietly at those who were now hiding between the large stones, which were scattered over the little hill. The creature saw them very well how they were hiding. None of the heroes had seen these creatures before.

After a few moments two of those birds also landed below, all staring at Efreu and at banits. The creatures were less interested in lizard, which certainly had met in the past. Up on the sky were two or three more of these great birds. The lizard people were frightened. They couldn't fight at this moment with these creatures. They surely would lost the battle, even if they were about forty, and the birds were only six. Any way, because the winged had no plans to attack them, the lizards stayed down quietly, hoping the birds will leave.

At one point a bird approached through Efreu. Hingus, Billy, and Emos were terrified. If the beast was going to kidnap Efreu, it could do it without any problem. The bird came nearer. The lizards left that area, leaving those whom they escorted without any defense. They didn't care if the creatures attacked and killed the heroes.

Billy stood up, and he positioned himself between the bird and Efreu. Emos, located slightly away from Efreu, also stood up and advanced toward the wise to protect him against that bird. But Efreu made a sign to Emos to sit back. Then he went through Billy and touched him softly with his hand and also made a sign to slowly sit down. After the giant sat down, Efreu advanced through the bird, and the bird advanced through him. Everything happened very quickly, but without any noise. Just a few moments passed until the bird was right in front of the wise. He stopped in front of the bird; it was immense.

Efreu slowly raised his hand to touch the bird. The bird leaned her large beak toward Efreu. It could easily swallow the prophet. The bird's beak approached the wise more and more, but before he could touch the creature, a powerful scream scared everyone. It was an awful sound, a bird's scream, a scream that was so close that feared everyone.

The birds flew in a second. The others did the same, and you could see clearly that the birds flew toward the top of the mountain.

The scream did not scare Efreu at all. The others stood up on their legs but with caution. All of them looked at how the birds left. Emos approached Efreu.

The wise answered at some question and thoughts, which had bothered Emos; Efreu said to the young, "The birds have left because they were called. I do not know who called them, but I heard the call. So I wasn't scared because someone spoke with me, and I heard his words."

But the silence was interrupted again, "Let'ss continue the trip!"

It was Reptoc. He commanded all his men to move. The lizards began to push our heroes to continue walking.

And all were set in motion again. They passed through the same narrow corridors again; after another steps away they went through some places where the road became a tunnel because the two walls were joined together. After another step they met again an intersection of corridors. If you are not familiar with the way they walked through, surely you could get lost.

After another few hours of walking through these corridors, they reached at last one very large opening. It was a very high plateau, an immense plateau. There were mant areas with small trees, high trees, and small imensialiss trees, with all kinds of great flowers and plants, with a luxuriant vegetation. These forests could hide all kinds of creatures. Even the largest creatures were able to hide into these woods.

"This is our location. We are not used to giving names to our city because they used to be destroyed pretty quickly."

Our heroes didn't see anything; Into that jungle you can't see anything. Only after another period of time did they see a small "something." It was a big rock with some lizards staying at an entrance. There was nothing sensational about this, only that these lizards were bigger than the archer lizards. These were full of muscle, two or three times bigger than them. Not taller, because they had only head more than the archers, but they were stronger. Stronger than Billy, Shigash, or Marnuk. Surely they could easily kill with his bare hands one of those from the horde. Maybe even Shigash could die if he'll fight with one of these creatures with bare hands.

The group entered that rock, and they began to climb down. On both walls were torches because after some steps the group was more and more inside the ground.

They also met some lizards that probably got out to hunt something to eat. They met other small groups, which probably were put there as guards.

Finally they had reached at some kind of settlement into the ground. There were dozens of big tents. There were also three buildings, with two floors, in which probably stood the lizard king and his captains. Perhaps their queen was also somewhere there.

"I have done my quest. Now you will be taken in front of our king. He will decide what to do with you," said Reptoc. Then he left . . .

Some lizard soldiers showed them the path to the building where their leader was. Indeed it was one of the largest. That was some wooden construction. And it also had protective walls built of wood. The gates were just some places without a wall. You could move quietly through them whenever you wanted—that is if you were in good relationships with those lizard people or, rather, if you were one of them. It seemed that these creatures were not in good relationships with other races.

Finally they entered into the building, which had two floors. The windows had uniform holes in the wall but not very carefully crafted. The group formed by banits, marnasits, and their companions stopped at the sign made by one of the soldiers. Another approached a door, knocked, and it opened in front of his eyes a little loophole; he talked to the one who was behind that door. The loophole closed after a few moments, and on the right side a heavy door was lifted. The gate was built out of metal bars, so you could see through them but could not pass unless someone would raise it.

The group climbed the stairs. There was only one door, in front of which stood four big reptiles. They were different reptiles like those who were guarding the entrance into the reptiles village, reptiles that looked more dangerous than these lizard archers. Creatures whose muscles can break down any of the group who came to visit their leader. With huge spears.

The door opened, and all entered the room, including the four guards. Without waiting for any sign, Shigash approached the lizard king and bended in front of him in respect.

The king was as big as an archer, but unlike the others, he was wearing some rare furs and some old talismans that were considered priceless jewels. In any case he looked like a king because he had a great crown, which was actually an increased cranial bone.

But surely there were other things that made him the king of these lizards. And probably we will see what those things are.

"Sshigassh, old friend," said the king icily. „So much time ssince we havn't sseen each other." While he was speaking, from time to time, he moved his split tongue in the air; easily you could see that he smelled the banits with it because besides that he also looked at them.

"Since me saved your life, not seen," said Shigash to that creatures.

"Yess . . . yess, I know," the reptile carelessly said. "But that wass long time ago. Now timess have changed."

"Hope you not forgotten. You promised when me saved your life that you return same liability. And me think time has come to—"

But he didn't finish his words. The lizard king spoke, "Let'ss ssee the niptuss," shamelessly interrupting. "Do not forget that you came here to fulfill the prophecy . . . or at least to try. Sso it'ss him."

He looked at the boy. He aproacched the boy and touched him with his tongue. But even if Billy was a little more afraid, he tried to not show that. But the reptile saw the boy's fear, and he smiled.

"Sso thiss iss the niptuss."

"Indeed," Shigash said. "But—"

"We know what bothered you. And we have the ssame problemsss. We will fight with you againsst the evil forcess, which are trying to destroy life on thiss planet. It'sss in our interesst to fight alongsside you and the forcess ssent to help by Lord of Light. But we'll talk about it after your return. We do not want to be sstruggling with our queen, but we can not ressisst becausse that'ss the dessire of the Creator."

"Thank you for these proper words," Efreu intervened.

But the reptile didn't hear anyone, maybe because he didn't want. He said again, "Then you shouldn't wait. You will be guided to the place where she is. We'll talk after that," said the lizard.

The soldiers forced the group toward the exit using physical force. Emos, Billy, and Hingus waited for a sign from Efreu, so they could also respond with force. But Efreu said calmly, "This is what it was written. Let's go and meet with that queen."

Coming out of the building but this time through the other side of the city, the group straightened toward the planet's inside. They walked a while, and finally they arrived to some ruins of an old fortress. The tower was still standing, which could collapse, and several pieces of the wall. Surely the fortress was once very big. Testimony were the pieces of wall that still stood up, and whom you saw scattered over a large area.

The young asked Efreu about this place, but he didn't know anything about this ancient settlement. Neither Shigash knew anything about it.

"I guess that's what they called Valley of the Complaint," said Efeu. It was once was a city of unprecedented splendor.

Discussion was quickly interrupted by a lizard man.

"Here we musst sstop."

It was a sort of entry into the earth. There were some stone steps. Maybe it was the basement of the former fortress that now lay in ruins.

"You have weaponss insside, right at the entrance, but I do not know how this will help you. But if ssomehow you manage to kill our queen, then bring with you a proof that you killed her. Sshe hass a talisman around her neck, which iss received from her ancesstorss. It hass great value for our king. Necessarily bring it to him, if you manage to kill the queen."

The heroes were forcibly pushed inside. Those lizard people were in a hurry. Something made them very nervous.

After all of them were pushed inside a cave, the heroes heard the sound of closing gate behind them, and those who were outside locked the gate. Then they heard a few boulders hitting the gate.

Anyone who was inside couldn't ever get out of here. Only if there was another exit somewhere else; otherwise, they were lost inside forever.

The heroes were trapped inside. Everywhere you look there were weapons and shields. And bodies also—lots of skeletons and bones. All kinds of skeletons from all kinds of creatures, big and amall creatures. Even lizard skeletons. Probably from those who were punished by the king.

And all these bodies, all these bones—something had devoured some of them. Many of them were eaten only in one meal. You can figure that because there were some places with lumps of bones. After they took the weapons and all they needed, they began to climb down the stairs. They were a little bit scared. They probably got used with the heavy trials, which always suddenly came; but after seeing so many deaths, they had the right to be scared.

Besides that, inside the cave you can hear all sorts of strong howls—many of them. The noise which have been produceing by the collapsed boulders over a metal gate, waked up from numbness all the souls that were in that underground cave.

Advancing more and more on that corridor, finally they reached a small room. It was a room of that huge cave. In the middle there was an elevator with a mechanism, built at the mouth of a perfectly vertical and very deep channel. Looking around, they realized that the only way they could go was through that channel. A pasageway was big enough, and an elevator could carry twenty people at once. So it was not a problem for all the heroes. The only problem was that they didn't know what they will encounter at the end of the vertical passageway.

After they inspected the mechanism a bit, all of them sat on that elevator. One of them touched a lever, and the elevator began to descend. Same time everywhere sat a grave silence . . . and dark . . . All those howls disapered in a second. Now everyone could hear the breath of the man beside him, an accelerated and agitated breath.

"Be prepared for any situation," Shigash whispered silently to the others, "because us not know what awaits down there."

"Master Efreu, what happens to your staff?" Rahnab asked. The boy was as high as Efreu's staff, and he could see bettter than anyone that something had happened with that scepter.

These words attracted the attention of all of them. That was a sign—and not exactly a good sign.

"You said that only when Voron's power is almost present that this staff will light," said Billy, scared.

"I know, but how is it possible? These lizard men have said they will fight with us, so there has to be another explanation," replied Efreu.

"Great Efreu, should be less confident in lizard creatures. They never chose right path. Me sure lizard creatures no plans help us."

"I know, Shigash," Efreu answered. "But part of my heart didn't want to believe such things. We all know that the king of the lizard people has requested that talisman from the queen's throat because he discovered that it is one of the keys to the Amnus. So he let us to struggle with it. If we win, then they will do everything to take that key from us, and—the only hope is to find all three keys to open the gates to get into Amnus town and try to defend our life from there. If we die here, we die with the last hope for those who came behind us. And the king knows this."

"Now we have to run from those lizards that surely are everywhere on surface and wait us to get out. Certainly we will meet them . . . if we escape from these places," said Billy, who seemed to be the most pessimistic person in every situation they had to face. The most pessimistic—or the most realistic?

"Have faith in our Lord, Billy," said Efreu to the young. "He will take care of what we cannot take care."

Only simple words? Or is there really someone who takes care of us, someone that helps us whenever we need Him that never should we lose our faith in Him?

These words somehow helped our heroes. It rose their spirits, even Billy's, knowing that someone was watching over them. Someone was taking care of their lives; a trace of hope sprouted in the heart of our heroes. Anyone would be more confident in his powers if he had little faith. And they did so. Faith was the only thing that could guide them to victory. And Efreu's role in this expedition was maybe the most important. He was the one that was supposed to infuse faith in everyone. If you have faith in yourself, then you can succeed more than you ever imagined.

"Everything depends on us . . . on our strength, and as wise Efreu said, what we cannot solve will be solved by our Creator," said Emos to strengthen Efreu's words.

Suddenly and finally they reached the end of that pasageway, and they dropped. Everything was lit up down there. It was a round room, which had four entrances placed one in front of the other. Any of these could send them in front of danger.

On the walls of the chamber were bronze sculptures. Some fight scenes of creatures with wings were represented on those walls. They attacked some groups of people dressed in white. People sised as the banits. But they were dressed like Efreu. And they also had staffs. They used those staffs to fight against those winged.

"This is battle between Harpyss and who once lived this city," said Shigash.

"It appears that they are losing the fight," said Hingus.

"This fight probably was sculpted to warn others," intervened Rahnab. "Others . . . like us."

"Like us," Emos and Hingus said at the same time, looking at the walls.

The child was near Efreu. He stood and watched at some signs,

which were almost erased. But if you looked more carefully, you could see something that certainly will attract the attention of our heroes.

On that piece of wall was a scene of someone dressed in a long shirt, standing in front of a giant dressed with a huge coat. And the giant from the scene was well armed. You also could see some images with some kinds of lizards on that wall: archers. But many scenes couldn't be read because they were erased. Many generations had died since those walls were sculpted.

"Wise Efreu, you and Shigash are appearing on this wall."

All of them came to look at that wall. None of them didn't say anything. They just looked at that wall for a while. What also got their attention was a picture of a huge creature or something with more than two arms. Maybe it's the queen, but none of them could say that for sure because the image was almost entirely erased from the wall.

Billy broke the silence, "What does it mean, and why were the next images removed from the wall? It's us, that's for sure, but you can't understand anything else. I saw those marnasits near us, but I also saw those lizards near them. And since the lizards haven't been so friendly with us, I'm starting again to believe that Shigash and the others are our enemies."

"Billy, Billy, only bad thoughts are in your mind. You think too much. And you have too little faith in the Creator. You should have more faith in Lord of Light. He will help us. You also need to think more how to purify the soul. You must banish the dark thoughts that cross through your mind."

It seemed that the real power of Efreu began to emerge. Or maybe it was the power of the Most High. Now he knew better than ever what thoughts bothered everyone. He knew how to encourage the others. And besides all that, his stick became green blue in color. This is for sure a sign that someone was with the heroes, assisting them in taking every decision, but it was also a sign that the evil forces were closer than ever.

"Anyway, what will happen depends on our Lord and depends on us. These sculptures maybe didn't show the reality of what will happen. What is certain is that Shigash and his people helped us a lot. And I'm sure that the Creator would show me if something is wrong about them. And Shigash also wants to help his people."

"He is so right," said Emos to the others. "They helped us a lot. And who can say for sure that in those sculptures the marnasits are against us?"

Silence.

"None of you!" completed Emos. "Even if in those pictures they are represented as fighting against us, I know that this couldn't be true because I saw what they have done for us! We must try to understand that we are same, one people. Even if we don't look the same."

Nobody was speaking now. Even Billy was looking down, knowing that he made a mistake. They helped them a lot.

"Not even great evil can separate us from what we love," Emos said again. But know he said this with sadness in his voice. He was thinking about Adela, his true love.

After some moments of profound silence, Shigash said something, "We are same. You see this in future. Until then us must aware of danger lurking this moment, this place."

He didn't finish his words, and the silence was broken by the same strong screams; only this time they were very close.

"Prepare your weapons, because we'll fight!" yelled Emos while he prepared his sword for battle.

"I have a spear for anyone who would dare to fight against us!" Hingus shouted.

Others, without saying anything, prepared their axes and swords. After they made several moves cutting the air, they stopped, keeping their weapon in a threatening position, ready to fight.

"My king, one you expect came," said a guard with a hard voice while he bent his body in front of his king.

"Let him in!" said the agitated king, using the same language specific to these reptiles. "And leave me alone with him. Out! All of you!"

The guards got out. But before they could bend as a sign of respect in front of their leader, "Out! Now!"

He was very nervous and scared at the same time. You can see clearly on his face, or rather by his gestures, because they could not draw their feelings on their faces. His movements were clumsier and fussier. Finally he sat on his throne and tried to make himself look more calmly.

The door opened, and a person dressed in armor from head to toe entered. He was as tall as the king of reptiles, and his stature was like a warrior from the horde. He made a lot of noise with his metal boots. The sword that was wrapped around his waist was so big that it also touched the floor, making a noise loud enough for everyone to hear. It was a noise that caused fear, especially in the silence of that room. The helmet covered his face entirely. But a very heavy breath sounded from his helmet when he stopped. He seemed not at all impressed by the king. It gave no importance to the king's rank; he didn't sketch any gesture of greeting in front of the lizard king, as the marnasits and the banits had. He didn't bend in front of the king.

But the truth is, looking at the king and how he trembled, there was no way to show him respect. He looked like a child waiting to be punished by his father.

A tough and very strong voice came out from under that helmet. It was a sound of a doomed soul.

"Dark Lord has sent me to see if you did as he commanded." Uz'Khal was the name of the one who came.

"I . . . I took care of everything . . . as ordered," said the king, very scared.

"Means they are down there now."

"Yes . . . down there, and the queen and her maids wait for them."

"There are several outputs in case they manage to kill your queen," said the voice again.

"Yes, but they can't get rid of our queen. They have no chance," the king spoke with confidence of his queen's strength. "Our queen is the most terrible being of our tribe. It's impossible for someone to—"

But he didn't finish his speech. The one with the armor said while he left the room, "Tell your people to show us where those outputs are. Now!"

After he got out, Reptoc with some archers got inside, and they waited for orders. They bent.

"Drive the captain at the four outputs of the temple where our queen leaves. Go there with him and take with you as many archers as you can. More than fifty at every output."

"I understand." Reptoc bent again in front of his king. And he looked fast and short at some officers. They got out immediately, accomplishing the orders.

Reptoc came easily near his king and asked, "It was him?"

"No," replied the leader. "It's one of his captains. It's his cavalry captain. Captain of the 665 riders. He is leading them."

"Didn't look so scary."

"He is not so scary," replied the king. But when he was alone with the cavalry captain before, he was scared then ever. Even now, he was very scared. But he could not show this to his men.

"But what I heard about him is very terrifying," Reptoc said.

But the king said nothing more about it. He only said, "Prepare all the troops for the journey that awaits us."

The lizard captain moved his head in sign of approval, and he left the room.

The doors of the throne chamber were closed, and the king remained alone. He meditated at all the things he must do in the next future. Surely he was thinking about what will hapen in the future, what he must do to be sure that everything will be best for his people.

"Aarnos!" Efreu cried to the youth. "Help Emos!"

Emos really needed help. Three harpiss struggled with him, some creatures that resembled those of women horde. But these creatures had some teeth that were stronger and fiercer; they were gifted with wings instead of arms and also with two strong claws instead of feet. Their fight was to fly quickly from side to side and attack with claws or with that mouth endowed with strong teeth.

Aarnos helped Emos. He jumped and hit one of those creatures so powerfully that it fell out of breath. Many harpiss fell, but even so their number was increasing as more and more of them appeared.

One of them hurt Hingus, although his spears were thrown with such precision that the harpiss couldn't approach. But even if he was wounded, Hingus passed from one victim to another. Heading for one of those fallen harpiss, which was lying down, he took the spears that got stuck in her heart and threw the spear in another flying creature, increasing the number of his victims.

Shigash, the giant, was in the midst of battle. Two winged creatures were caught in the fur on his back. One of them was trying to bite his neck, but Shigash caught her and threw to the ground with tremendous force. His two-edged axe was lost somewhere, so he had to fight with bare hands. He was also hurt, as well as Hingus and the others, but those were some injuries that could not beat such warriors. Those were some superficial injuries for them. But they were tired because of the attacks of those winged. So the torment became more difficult.

"Hingus!" shouted Aarnos to his companion. "Please help Rahnab."

The little Rahnab really needed help. Although he was armed with one of Hingus's spears, he did not have the necessary strength to fight with a flying creature. A harpiss, taking advantage of his weakness, broke the javelin with a strong bite and hit the young man with such power that the boy fell down injured. Maybe it was worse than a simply injury, but nobody could see what really happened to the boy.

But before the harpiss could touch the boy again, a spear came from Hingus with such power that it pierced the winged and stuck in the chamber's wall. The gift from Emos, the top of those spears, was indeed the best. The spears were able to penetrate the wall just like flesh.

"This is what you deserve if you hurt a helpless child!" yelled Hingus.

Seeing his brother down, Aarnos cried very loud and burst into the sight of a group of harpiss that attacked Efreu, Emos, and the others. Shigash had fallen with three winged over him. Marnuk was trapped in a corner and tried to defend himself with his hammer but also couldn't do much to protect himself. None could help him or others. And all of them needed help.

There were only about two dozen winged, but their strength was great. They were more than our heroes; some of our group were attacked by three or four harpiss. And our heroes were scattered everywhere, so they couldn't fight side by side. Our hero's chances were smaller than ever. Like I said, even Shigash was hurt and thrown down by these creatures. Hingus, Emos, and Efreu also were lost, even Billy after he began to attack those winged with such power. He succeeded to hit one or two of them, but after that, three harpiss sent him down to ground. And they began to bite the giant with their sharp teeth.

But suddenly something came to help them. When all seemed lost, when the end was near for our heroes, they heard a sonorous voice, a deep voice that was very strong. It also sounded like a whisper but said in a loud voice.

"Who dare disturb me from my sleep!? Who dare disturb me?"

The struggle between heroes and those harpiss stopped. The winged stopped and watched toward the direction wherefrom the voice had come. They were very frightened, especially because when the voice began to speak, the other access corridors were closed with some huge bars. Surely that some of them had met that creature in the past. Now the only thing they could do is to go ahead toward their only access way, wherefrom that voice came, a voice that seemed to be bothered and unhappy because of the noise caused by the fight. Or they could stay and expect that creature to come.

It seemed that those harpiss already took the decision to retreat. Although it was clear that they didn't have the courage to pull through that passage to fight with the creature that was approaching, they eventually took the decision to go in that direction. They began to fly toward that voice.

It was about this time that everyone take a decision about the next moves because the creature's shadow was visible now. From a ramification of that corridor, from somewhere near the left side, appeared a shade that couldn't be clearly seen. But by the size of that shadow, I could tell you it was a very large beast.

Harpiss approached more and more by the loopholes of that corridor. But when they began to fly every one where it could, each trying to save its life, right that moment there appeared that creature. Some of the winged continued their way farther along the aisle and disappeared into the other inputs that could be found along the corridor. Others flew straight ahead through the entrance where the monster had appeared. But two of them hadn't been so lucky. The beast that was at least five times taller than the harpiss and barely managed to stay straight in that corridor that was too tight for her trapped these two harpiss in one of her six arms. She threw one of them onto the wall until that harpiss became a rag. Then she threw the corpse into the direction where the heroes were. The other was maybe a little lucky as it had not met the same cruel death. If the one caught by the beast in her arm cried sharply until she gave her last breath, the second harpiss was cut in half by one sword, which the beast had. I say one because that creature had three huge long swords as big as Shigash's and a mace in the fourth one. The other two arms were free, but this does not mean they were less dangerous.

The heroes remained in that place where they fought with the winged. It was perhaps the best decision. First, there was more room in that chamber, second Rahnab was wounded and unconscious, and third they had enough time to "talk" with that creature.

The beast came closer and closer. Now it was possible to discern all the details of that creature. She was so big, with six strong arms. Her face was like a woman's face. But it was a cruel and very old face. She had long hair and a crown above her head that strongly shone. It was a precious metal, decorated with some extremely rare and precious stones. But what really got the heroes was that the beast had no legs. Instead of legs, her body continued to a very high and voluminous tail, and the creature was staying on that tail, using it to move her body.

"It seems like this is queen," Shigash whispered.

"I expected her to be a little higher," Hingus tried to raise his comrade's courage.

"I hope . . . I hope she has fewer arms," Emos said slowly.

The two young boys looked at each other and smiles. At least all the group was now reunited, and they could help each other. It couldn't be worse to fight against one creature than fighting with twenty.

Everyone took his weapon. Only Rahnab was still unconscious.

"Are you all right? Efreu asked the fighters, looking at Rahnab, who was thrown on the floor.

All the heroes were injured, but none of them were complaining. They were true warriors.

Efreu looked at each one, and they signaled that they were ready to fight.

The creature began to move. Although Efreu and others, especially Aarnos, wanted to go and see what happened to the little boy, this was impossible because the creature was quickly approaching. Even if she didn't have legs but a snake-like tail, she quickly crossed almost the entire distance between her and those who were waiting for her.

"A smell that I have not felt for many years. These little ones are very tasty," said the queen, looking with lust especially at Rahnab, who lay fainted on the ground.

"We do not let you to get closer," cried Aarnos.

"We'll see." The queen laughed.

"None of us will ever let you touch him. Rather, we die than let you touch him," cried Hingus.

"I like to fight for my prey. And about your death, I think it wouldn't be a problem."

Outraged, Hingus threw one of those spears he had. He threw with such force and anger that he got all his friends by surprise. The spear was meant to that cruel queen, who seemed to have met banits somewhere in the past. Long ago, probably when the banits had the habit to roam the world.

Hingus threw that spear to take the victim by surprise. But he was the one who was taken by surprise. The queen couldn't be tricked. She caught the spear thrown by the young without any difficulty. She then threw the spear in the other free arm, and then she threw it with an even greater power over Shigash. Without realizing what had happened to him, he dropped his double-edged axe from his hand, and he shouted with all his strength because of the pain. Then, because he couldn't stand up any longer on his feet, he crumbled onto the ground. That special spear made by Emos from a tough metal after an old recipe from his ancestors penetrated the thick fur, which protected Shigash in all the battles he had fought before.

The giant had now fallen to the ground. One of the best fighters was hurt without ever having anything to say. Aarnos's brother, Rahnab, also was lying unconscious, perhaps seriously injured or even dead, behind them. The heroes had to deal with a beast that had proved it is much stronger than any opponent they had met before. They had to fight with this creature and must protect Shigash and Rahnab.

"Spread out so we can protect Rahnab and Shigash! Keep them behind us . . . behind us all the time! Do not let this beast to get near them!" shouted Efreu to the others.

Marnuk and the other two marnasits—silent as always, obedient to the orders only from their master Shigash—had listened to Efreu, and they sat in three parts of that beast to attack her. They had taken a strategic position to defend not only their boss but the boy too. Perhaps the idea of unity, the idea of fighting together for success, was finally understood. At least by them.

Hingus threw again a spear in the same manner as the last time. This time, that huge target also grabbed the spear and threw it toward one of the three who were part of the horde. Fortunately, this time the queen missed her target. The spear had penetrated the shield of the marnsit, a strong shield made by the skin of a beast they had killed.

"Hingus, stop throwing spears!" cried Emos with despair in his eyes.

Hingus looked frightened at his friend, then at wise Efreu. The old man said to him with a slow voice, "Stop throwing."

All were scared. Even those from the horde knew that none of them were so skilled in handling spears as Hingus. And they never had to face such strong creatures. If those spears thrown from a distance couldn't hurt that queen, what else could they do with their axes and spears? And now without Shigash and without Hingus's spears, their chances of success were rapidly decreasing.

Scared of what he had seen, Hingus was armed with one of his spears, but this time he was prepared to use it only to defend himself and his friends. Now the heroes were more than one group of people. Even if there were disagreements between them, those who had started the search of Amnus gates keys were now friends. Yes, friends.

But let's return to our fight. Shigash was now down trying somehow to break the spear that pierced him. The spear had entered through him by front and got out on the other side. But the giant couldn't succeed because his powers were increasingly weakened. Also the pain was increasing. The others saw he was becoming weaker but could not do anything.

"You are all dead!: said that horrible voice again. "Which one of you should I send first among his ancestors?" laughed the frightening creature while she always moved her body in the left and right side. Even though the queen was very high and had no legs to move, she had a surprising reaction at speed. She turned on all sides, always ready to defend herself against those who had surrounded her. She looked carefully at all of them. She lived a long life, probably several hundred years, and all this time made her a strong opponent against any creatures.

Lizard queen's eyes were directed toward the people who were part of the horde maybe because they were the biggest. Billy was massive too, but because he always stayed next to his brother, the queen didn't seem disturbed by him.

And so the beast picked her next victim. She approached Marnuk quickly and attacked him with a force worthy of her stature. Luckily Marnuk was strong and had a great hammer, or else from beginning of the attack, he would have lost. Another one in his place maybe would not have done so well. Three arms, each of them with a sword in hand, fell upon Marnuk without interruption. A fourth arm also struck him with power, holding a big axe. That rain of hits almost destroyed Marnuk. He became so tired because of that. Hardly could he parry such strikes, although the attack had begun only a few moments ago.

Another man from the horde, Ormath, jumped to help Marnuk. In fact, all of them were ready to attack and help, but Ormath was the closest to that creature than anyone so he was able to attack the queen with his mace with a metal handle, thick as the arm of a banit, continuing with a chain nearly as thick as the handle and in the end with some spikes as large as those canines that went out of his mouth. He managed to hit that queen.

"You will regret that you hit me! You'll regret that you came here!" cried the creature.

"Pull up, Ormath!" shouted Marnuk while continuing to defend the shots.

But it was too late. Hurt by Ormath, the queen turned and caught him with both arms. And now the poor marnasit was lifted a few feet above the ground. He was lost in the arms of that creature. The queen also continued to attack Marnuk. The same interrupted rain of hits was thrown away over Marnuk. So the queen could handled with these marnasits at the same time. Actually she was fighting with Billy too. So she could fight with all three warriors at the same time. When Billy attacked her with his weapon, the queen crossed two swords and parried the hit—hardly is it true, but this was only because Aarnos's power couldn't be challenged by anyone, even by her. But she also had been surprised by this attack because she must fight with all three of them at the same time. She succeeded in defending against the young, and then she hit him with the body of Ormath. The two lurched and rolled until they hit their bodies on the wall of that room. They were seriously injured because of that. Even Efreu was thrown somewhere by the queen's tail. But even so, both of them were back on their feet. You could see that on their faces and moves. When the beast was fighting with Marnuk, Ormath, and Billy, Efreu was hurt; and he couldn't get back on his feet so quickly like Billy and Ormath. It was a tough hit.

Seeing his teacher down, Emos attacked the queen with his sword. And if Hingus was the best fighter with spears, Emos was the greatest with a sword. I didn't see anyone like him. With so much grace, he avoided the queen's strikes and cut her with his swords. The queen tried to hurt Emos with all her heart, but she couldn't. The young boy was much too agile. His sword was so easy to use by a man like him. And the queen didn't touch him but probably because Emos quickly withdrew from the battle with her. Even if he was a great warrior, he couldn't fight with her without the help of the others. And the others couldn't help him right now. I think they couldn't face again an attack like this. In a few moments the queen almost seriously injured Ormath, Marnuk, Billy, and Efreu. Shigash was also injured. Only Emos and the other marnasit, Cael, weren't hurt by this beast.

"Who should I attack now?" the queen asked while laughing and looking at Marnuk. "Maybe I will attack you again!" she said while looking at Marnuk. "Or should I attack you . . . for my own pleasure," said the beast to Cael. "Or should I get rid of these fresh bloods?" she addressed the banits. "You caused me many troubles with all your attacks." She looked at Emos too, but she didn't say anything about him. Even he hurt her, she couldn't say anything about him in front of the others. Even if Emos was a great warrior, she couldn't approve with that. Such a queen couldn't be afraid of someone like him, someone so small compared with her. But if at the beginning of the battle the queen thought that the most dangerous could be only the marnasits, now she realized that an opponent never should be underestimated.

"But I think I will take of the child first! And then I will come after you!" she said.

But after she had finished her words and even before she had prepared to attack Rahnab, Efreu said to her, "How dare you oppose to the Lord of Light? How dare you? Leave us and go back into the darkness from which you came!"

"A-ha . . . a hamaan . . . a hamaan commands me! I should know that even if you look older, you're not. You're acting too well after such a hit. I will take care of you after I'll take care of child."

Others did not understand what the two were talking about. Efreu was with them for a long time, since Emos was a little boy, while his parents were alive. It's true that nobody knew where he came from or where he lived until he settled in the city of Megos. But neither of them asked him that. But everything became clearer now. It will. It appeared that this creature knew who Efreu was or rather what he was. A hamaan, whatever that meant. He knew him and his own people.

The creature was going to attack Rahnab. She was heading toward Rahnab with high speed. But in those moments Efreu's staff was mindful with a large force. Something—a bright light— seemed to take birth on top of that staff. And not only was it born, but it sent a wave of fire and struck out the queen in one of her arms. While he sent the fire against the creature, Efreu cried out, "In the name of the Almighty, I punish you!"

The lizard queen was hit pretty badly now. Her arm was bleeding. She changed her direction, and she was heading to Efreu. But another wave of fire wounded the queen somewhere in her chest. After this, the creature stopped.

"If you won't go away and leave us alone, you'll be hit again by anger of the Most High! You will be hardly hit by His wrath!" yelled Efreu.

All our heroes were very amazed. Even Shigash was so amazed by what he saw that he forgot the anguish of his wounds.

This help that came from Efreu was everything they needed. They could finally get some rest now.

The beast was sitting and thinking about something. He thought about what she should do next. What seemed at first an easy fight for her now became a heavyweight fight. The one who seemed the most powerless in front of her seemed to be strongest at this moment.

"Kill her!" said Marnuk.

"Yes, kill her!" said Hingus.

Everyone now stood and watched Efreu and the great beast—a beast who, after causing them so many problems, was now at Efreu's mercy. They were waiting for an answer from Efreu or at least one move from him, maybe even to kill the creature.

"I cannot," replied Efreu slowly. "Prophecy says that only Rahnab, the niptus, can kill her. What is written must be fulfilled exactly because this is the will of our Lord."

"Maybe she will find a way to destroy us, even you, Efreu, if we don't kill her," said Billy while he was trying to see how Rahnab was. It was hard to see the child because while they were fighting, the beast placed herself in a way that she was keeping Rahnab on her back side, so none could see him.

"My staff lost his strength. Only if she is trying to attack us again, only then it will recover its power and I will be able to touch her again. And—"

But he was interrupted by the lizard creature.

"I'll let you out of here. You are free to get back on the way you came," said the queen. And the door before them was now opened. Everyone looked at each other. Even if the door was now open, to them, it was impossible to leave Shigash and Rahnab behind. And besides, they still needed the charm on her neck. We shouldn't forget about the medallion. For those who came after them, that charm was the most important thing. Their salvation.

But only a second of disregard was what she needed so she could disappear. While they were looking at that gate, which was opened, the queen took Rahnab and quickly disappeared in one of those corridors. The group began to run after her, but once again those harpiss attacked our heroes.

The winged were fewer in number. And they couldn't face such bitter warriors. They didn't want to lose the queen and their niptus. Even Efreu's rod was again mindful of that divine force. The fire came out from the scepter and hit the harpiss; the creatures fell down without being able to retaliate in any way. Billy cut the winged with his axe, Hingus threw his spears, and the winged fell down like flies. Emos also was doing everything possible to save the child's life. Even Marnuk cried so loudly because he couldn't stop the queen and save Rahnab. He ran like mad, killing the entire creature he met in front of him. All the heroes were doing everything they can to save Rahnab.

But because of those harpiss, the heroes slowed. So the queen was getting farther; they could see now only a big shadow moving very fast. As if this wasn't enough, a great iron gate closed in front of them. They became more aggressive. All the harpiss that remained were killed in cold blood very quickly. But this wasn't enough. The queen's intention was achieved. Rahnab was kidnapped, taken to a place where heroes could not reach, and would probably be killed. Or probably he was already dead, or worse, he could meet Voron himself.

Aarnos caught with his hands the bars and tried to break them. He was acting like a mad man. He didn't say anything—at least something with meaning. He growled something, but none could understand that. The marnasits also hit those bars with their great weapons, but this didn't help at all. So all of them looked toward the place where the queen disappeared. All were quiet. Who knew what they were thinking in those moments? But it is sure that you can see fear, despair, and pain on their faces.

The others sought a way to enter in that corridor leading to the throne room, but it was impossible. The only way to step into that corridor was a lever that should be lifted up. But the problem was that the lever was on the other side of gate. Hingus and Emos ran and bounced all around, trying to find another way to get inside.

But they were disappointed of what they discovered; it looks like that was the only mechanism that could open the gate.

There was a deep silence. A hellish peace. Probably everyone would want to fight for hours with that creature or with those harpiss than being in such situation like they were now. The boy was alone with the creature, and they could not do anything about it. It was devoid of any power, of any chance to fight, and moreover, he was unconscious. Even if the boy didn't say or do anything after he was hit, even if he was with the queen and he wouldn't have any chance against her, the heroes didn't want to believe anything else that the boy was only unconscious and everything will be fine with him.

All the heroes stood and waited for a miracle to save Rahnab. A sign from Lord of Light that should protect and save the child. Surely the sign will come. But why it outlasted so much.

Suddenly, the silence that swept all the rooms and corridors of the basement was interrupted by the scream of a child frightened to death. The sound was not very long but said it all. It was the sound of death. Whoever pulled off this sound was lost, especially because this sound was from a child. None of those fierce warriors could struggle with that queen of lizards, so a child could do less than that. Tears began to pour on the faces of those who knew what had happened. It is impossible to remain untouched by the feeling of pain when you face such moment when a helpless child loses his life. What kind of justice is this? Where is the Lord now?

Aarnos was destroyed. Words cannot express what he felt in that moment. How can you describe what you feel when you lose someone you love? Couldn't you do anything to prevent this? You shed your anger on those who are around you? You shed your anger on the Creator? You blame Him for all these?

Many of these thoughts went through Aarnos's mind. He felt so powerless. He felt that he could do more to protect his little brother. He could be more determined to stop Rahnab in coming with them. But even so, how could the Lord let someone kill such an innocent little boy? Isn't the kingdom of heaven theirs? He did not deserve to live more than anyone?

"Why should he have to die? Why him?" said Billy between his tears. And he tried to break once again the bars like mad.

At such question you really cannot respond somehow. It would be cruel of you try to say something to the one who is suffering, if you say that everything will be fine.

"Why?"

Everyone was still looking the grid, perhaps hoping that the Most High will still do something to save Rahnab. But no visible shadow movement could be seen from the place where the child and Queen had left. Only some silent noises.

"Help," came a little voice from the other side of the grilled gate.

But nobody heard it. Or at least none wanted to hear it. In such moments you can have visions; you can hear voices. Or probably I think I heard something. Probably it was a noise from the queen.

"Aarnos!" sounded that voice again but this time louder and with loud crying. "Aarnos, where are you!? Where are you?"

Now everybody was paying attention to the other side. They were looking frightened toward the place wherefrom the voice was coming. They were wrong! The boy was really alive? It was impossible for all of them to hear the same, But first they looked at each other to be sure that they all heard something. All were happy but also frightened because the beast could also hear him and return to kill the boy. And they couldn't face again such pain.

"I cannot lose him again. I need to do something," Aarnos said while running like a madman, looking for another great goal. "We should help him," he spoke so silently because he was afraid that the creature could hear him.

All the heroes became nervous and agitated; this might be their only chance. Probably the Lord gave them this chance. They now can see the shadow of the child. He was coming to them. Only if he can come more quickly.

"I'm here," said Aarnos to the boy. "We are here," he whispered.

A small figure came closer and closer. At the beginning they only saw shadows, but after a few moments, they saw the child.

Seeing the group at some moment, the boy ran to them as fast as he could.

"Aarnos!", he said when he saw his brother. And he took Aarnos's hands in his hands. "I'm afraid."

Aarnos smiled to him, but he looked at him for only a second. His eyes were looking at the place where the queen could come from. The others raised their weapons and shields, and they were prepared to give their lives for the little boy.

"Rahnab, you have to go backward and let down that lever," Efreu quietly said to the child. All of them were still agitated even if they already saw the boy. Danger was just one step away from them.

Aarnos pushed the boy a little roughly with his hands and showed him where to go. He wanted to see his brother on the same side.

"Go, Rahnab, go," whispered the others.

The boy, seeing them all so scared, became more scared. He went near the lever and let all his weight on it. That silence was broken by the noise generated by the moving of the lever. It was like a thunderstorm hitting a mountaintop. But the lever was stuck, and the gate didn't open. It began to open, but not even the child could get through that breach.

"I can't move it," said the little boy. And he ran near his brother again.

Aarnos looked at the boy, then at the room where the boy came from. Then he looked again at the child. The others were also very agitated and scared. They were trying somehow to open the gate, but not even the marnasits could move it.

"Rahnab, you must try," said Aarnos again, this time squeezing his brother's arms, as if he was never going to see him again. "You should try harder," he said.

The boy went near that lever again; looking very scared, he looked at the others agan, and then he began to push that lever, this time jumping on it. And it seemed that the press was working because the lever went down increasingly, making more noise. The others were all concerned.

When the lever was down for good, the grid began to climb up. Aarnos and those who were accompanying him made signs to the boy to run toward them. The boy began to run. And when he was close to his older brother, Billy caught his arm, Emos the other arm, and both of them pulled him toward them without even expecting the door to open totally.

Aarnos embraced his brother a little, almost suffocating him; and after that, all the heroes prepared themselves for battle. They had to kill that beast. They needed that key.

"What are you doing?" asked the boy when he saw that all the heroes were preparing theirs weapons, ready to defense themselves.

They were very afraid—all of them—even Efreu and the marnasits.

"We're preparing for another fight," Efreu answered.

"Us wait enemy kill it . . . destroy it," Marnuk said.

"But there's nobody," answered the child.

But without any of them returning because of what the boy said, Emos said to Rahnab, "Even if the queen left you alone for a few moments, she will return to look for you everywhere; we must be prepared," said Emos who was ready with his sword in one hand and with the shield in front of his body to protect himself against a possible attack.

"But the queen is dead," replied the innocent little boy.

Hearing these words, all the fighters couldn't remain as indifferent as before. They turned around and watched the boy. They were all amazed.

"What did you say, boy?" Efreu asked.

"I killed her myself. I didn't want that," replied the boy, as he expected to be punished for what he had done.

Aarnos approached his brother looking at him without any smile. He couldn't say anything to him. Efreu asked the boy.

"How did you kill her?" he asked him, like he was waiting for some more serious evidence. That creature, which gave them so many problems, couldn't be killed so easily by a child only. It couldn't be so easy for them.

"That beast grabbed me into her arms. I do not know what it was going to do to me. But before she has taken me in her arms and ran with me, I got the top of the spear that was near me. When she saw that I was no longer passed out, she tried to bite me so she brought my body to her mouth, to kill me. I think that is what she wanted to do to me. So I pulled the spear into her mouth. She screamed. I saw blood coming from her mouth, and she fell down. I think she died. After that, I came here. I have also got this thing from her neck." And he showed them the key to Amnus's city gate. The boy said all these words almost without breathing.

The group of adults didn't know what to say. All became silent. They stared at one another. They stared at the talisman. But nobody said anything. What more proof do they need? They had the key.

The boy offered the medallion to Efreu. The wise took it, and he looked at him with attention. He looked at the others, and he started to laugh. The others laughed too. Like all of them were crazy. The boy was the only one that did not laugh.

Efreu, as a response to all his questions, said, "We laugh because we didn't expect everything to come out so well. What was a burdensome for us proved to be something simple for you. Thank you for helping us, and thank you for helping those who come after us. You are a true fighter." And the old man made a reverence as a sign of respect for Rahnab.

Everyone else followed Efreu's example.

"You really niptus. You have my respect," said Marnuk, the warrior.

After this ritual in which the child was recognized as a great fighter, Efreu said, "Thank you, king of all heavens. Thank you for your strength, which is with us."

After a short silence, he continued, "Now let's go back to Shigash and Olaf and leave this place full of evil and thirst for blood."

After he said this, all of them went back toward the place where Shigash and Olaf were.

Olaf didn't know what to think when he saw his friends coming. He was losing any hope. He was prepared for any attack to protect his leader Shigash, but he knew that he couldn't do anything against such creature like the queen was.

But now when he saw his friends again, he rose up to his feet and saluted them with great respect. Even Shigash, who was so badly injured, tried to salute them with the same respect. He tried to stand up, but he couldn't. You can see on his face that he was suferring. When Olaf saw that Shigash was trying to stand up, he jumped and helped him. Shigash put his hand on his shoulder, and finally he stood up. He saluted his friends, and they all embraced each other: banits with banits, marnasits with marnasits, and banits with marnasits.

They succeeded in drawing out that spear from Shigash's shoulder; they needed to get out from that basement of the fortress. The exit on which they had come through, the road on which they had entered into those caves, was locked. So they must find another way to get out.

Anyway the air was easier to breathe in this part. It was cleaner. It was an evidence that they had chosen the right path. As they walked toward the exit, the banits asked Efreu what a hamaan was.

"We are the ones that were saved after the first resurrection," he said Efreu, "as the Book of Books said."

"So there are more like you?" Rahnab asked when he heard what Efreu was, looking at him with more admiration than before.

"Yes," replied Efreu, "and we are waiting for the second resurrection, those who have praised the Most High throughout their lives, those have inherited the eternal life and are now 'soldiers of light.' Before, when more of such events took place on other planets, more distant than the sun, those who were chosen by the Most High became 'soldiers' and sat near His throne. But since the Dark Lord Voron became stronger and stronger, more powerful than one's mind can imagine because he sent all his soldiers and creatures from everywhere in this universe, since then the Creator has commanded us to fight for those who deserve it.

Try to save them and their soul, even with the price of our soul. Things have become more complicated now. Much more difficult then the beginning of the universe. You can be saved now and become the soldier of light, but if you will be killed by the power of darkness, you'll become one of them. A creature that wants only war and death, there will be more wars. More will follow this one on other planets, and those who will come out victorious in the name of the Most High, in the war against Voron, will be saved. And they will fight in other wars against the Dark Lord, wars which will be on other planets. There will be wars as long as there is an enemy of the Creator. So Voron must be destroyed, and that day must be sooner. As sooner as better, because Voron's strength increases with age. His armies are more powerful and more numerous than ever. And they will grow. If we do not hurry to destroy him, then maybe we will lose this fight, and the other people from other planets will be lost forever. And the universe will be filled with fear, destruction, and death. And we cannot let this happen. We must win this war."

Efreu was speaking to his friends about a long war. A war that may take centuries until the end. All of them wanted to become warriors of the Creator because the damage done by the armies of Voron was too much painful. To see dying children and dying elderly and women was a too much painful for everyone. The only way to solve these problems was to destroy once and for all the one that for thousands of years, for tens of thousands of years, he persecuted the living beeing, those who had faith in the Most High.

"What happened there?" Shigash asked, interrupting the conversation between Efreu and banits.

"I hope it's our help," Efreu said with a smile.

You can hear all kinds of shouts. Our heroes were afraid because they could hear noises from the underground maze exit, which were not very friendly. They also could hear sharp screams, like the eagles'. Some shouts could easily put fear into anyone who heard them whitout even seeing the creature.

Fear became more deep when the heroes were close to that maze's exit. Even Efreu was scared, especially when he saw one of those lizard people approaching them. But the lizard didn't see them because he was busy with what was happening outside. Hingus prepared one of his spears to kill the lizard, but when he was ready to throw that spear in his enemy, something suddenly came up from the sky to the cave entrance and kidnap the man lizard. Seeing this, Efreu told the others, "Let's hurry! Let's go to the exit! Our help sent by the Most High are here, but we must be careful. Our enemies are also outside!"

Fight after fight—here lies the life of a person. On Mania it was the same, like everywhere as a matter of fact. You can only succeed through life by fighting, a fight witout breathing, with only a few moments of rest. But nobody can do anything about this. Not even the hamaans.

Preparing their weapons, the heroes started to run toward the exit. Reaching out, they were amazed at the two groups that were fighting outside. On one side were those lizard people, which they met before. They were upset about seeing them alive. How was it possible?

On the other side were Efreu's brothers. They were those who glorified the Creator all their lives. Now they are called hamaans. They were "soldiers of light," those who received the commandment from the Most High to fight against the armies of Voron the Dark Lord.

But this camp, when saw that the heroes were unharmed, unlike the lizards, they were very happy.

"Look at those who are marked with the power of the Creator. Those that can save this planet. We must protect them," shouted one of the hamaans. It seemed he was the leader of those who fought there against the lizard people. He stood on the body of one of those flying creatures that our heroes encountered when they went to meet with that lizard king. Throwing his stick fire waves, he brought havoc among those lizard people.

But even those hideous creatures created some serious injuries between the hamaan people. At the entrance of the cave and a little far from it were a few of such birds falling on the ground. Right in the moment when the heroes were at the mouth of those entrance, thirty to forty lizard archers gathered in a group, shooting arrows toward a hamaan. Since they were syncronized and very good archers, the lizards managed to hit the target in any situation. Even if the bird flew erratically, first to the left and then to the right, the archers hit the winged archers all the time. They did not even moved their bodies or heads. Their eyes and arms were always moving. The eyes were always directed toward the target, moving independently from one another, like the chameleon's, and with theirs arms they sent down the victim. Yes, the victim, because even these huge kinds of birds could not escape from them. With many injuries caused by the arrows, the bird still floated a little and then crashed out of breath.

The hamaan that flew with the bird survived because he was defended by the bird's wings. All the time when the archers pointed their arrows toward the hamaan, the birds put her wings like a shield against those arrows. Many arrows were rejected by the wind made with these wings, but some of them had hit the birds. But even if the bird was hit, the master was protected. Such enormous sacrifice for the master! Death!

But although the hamaan was not hurt, because of the speed of collapse and because the bird rolled many times, it certainly needed some time to get on his feet. The group of archers now was seeking another target. But another hamaan sitting on one of those birds hit a stone with a fire wave. The fire was so powerful that the stone fell over the lizards, killing almost all of them.

Among the victims were also some hamaans killed by the archers. They were lying on the ground breathless. Some of their wounds were very visible; five to six arrows were stuck in their bodies. Those giant birds killed by lizard people had dozens, perhaps hundreds, of such arrows in their bodies. There were quite many soldiers of light that had fallen to the ground. But there were about hundred times more dead lizard archers. It seemed that the battle was lost for them. Their forces were now significantly reduced. Some archers tried to save themselves. They still were a serious threat for the hamaans. But after seeing that their fight was not in vain and the heroes had survived such terrible hardships, the hamaans fought more powerfully.

Our heroes also joined their cause; they began to fight against the lizard men. These enemies now had to retaliate against those who killed the queen. Swords and axes now cut in the flesh of those creatures. The iron cut deeply into their flesh, causing many injuries and victims. Powerful flames, lightnings as strong as the flames, came out of the hamaans' scepters, hitting with cruelty their enemies. Other hamaans had other powers hidden in their scepter. Some could lift up huge boulders, throwing them on lizard people; others lifted up the archer reptiles, then throwing them into the mountain ravines. It was clear that those lizard people were defeated. Those who escaped, few in number, ran to the laps of Amnus Mountain. There were some places where you can see white substances. It was snow, but they never saw snow. The banits never saw such a thing. Also it was a little colder here. The banits and the lizards were not used with it. But the hamaans and the marnasits had no problem with this.

Walking through those caves and searching for the escape tunnels, they went over to the top of the mountain. But even if they climbed so much, they weren't at the middle of that mountain because it was extremely high. The dense forests that were close to the foot of the mountain, lakes full of freshwater, and swamps the heroes had passed through in their journey were no longer in these places. Instead there were trees with snow on them, but they were much smaller than those giants called imensialiss. The leaves of these trees were smaller and were different from those of the large trees. The imensialiss's leaf was much bigger than one banit, and it could hold good a banit or a marnasit on it; actually the heroes in their journey slept on those leaves. But the leaves of these trees of this new place were generally smaller, like those of coniferous trees. The waters here were frozen. It was like in a fairytale, a white landscape mixing with the browns of trunk of trees and their green leaves. The banits and the marnasits were amazed by what they saw.

The one who seemed to be the leader of that group of hamaans came down with the bird near Efreu and his companions. The others also did the same. Those who were already on the ground approached the group of the newcomers.

"Welcome," said approaching the leader, then addressing only to Efreu, "The eighteen kings will be happy to see that the one who was missing from his throne returned unharmed. And he brought with him hope, one of the keys of the city of Amnus."

After these words, the leader of that group of soldiers of light bowed his head as a sign of respect. The others followed his example.

"I'm glad I'm back. I missed this landscape and its inhabitants. Even if it's a hard time and I hoped I won't came back with such bad news, I'm happy to see all of you. My job was above my pleasure and joy, so I couldn't visit you as I wished. But I have been accomplishing my tasks . . . at least part of it. But only with the help of these heroes. We need some more keys to open the gate of Amnus."

"If you mean the other two keys, you should know that one of them is in our hands. And the other one, well, you have to climb a little higher, toward the top of the mountain. But the important things is that we know where it could be found."

These words made our heroes very happy. Finally fate smiled at them, or better said, the help of the Lord was not a long wait. It is true that they must find one more key—which could also be a difficult procedure, even more difficult—but at least they had the other two. For the third key, they had to go farther toward the direction they already had taken. At least they didn't have to go back where they could be forced to fight again with such danger. Perhaps, besides those dangers, the army of Voron would also be there. Those people, the lizards, it looked like they had chosen their allies: those forces of the Lord of Darkness.

"But our problem is to help those who come after us," Efreu said. And he sighed.

"Behind you," told Bhartolomeu, the leader, "are only the armies of Voron and lizard people because the lizards are allied of the Lord of Darkness. And their number is also very high . . . thousands of archers—very good archers."

"Where are our brothers then, those from our nation?" Emos asked, scared.

The marnasits were also scared. Their wives and children were also in that group. The last people from both nations were in that group.

"They are on the Nesus shelf. Where is our location? Some of our brothers were sent by the king to find you. Instead, they found the people of your nations. Then they escorted them to the Nesus Plateau where they are safe . . . at least until Voron's armies will appear. Reptiles have no chance to get there. Two stone walls, very tall form the only corridor that leads to our settlement. And on these two walls are many observation points. And not just observation but also defense points. No army can get through there. None besides Voron's army. That army can get easily through our defense. Only Amnus City can save us. Amnus City and the Lord of Light," continued Bhartolomeu.

"Means that we can meet with those whom we left behind a few days ago?" asked Hingus.

"We'll meet our parents?" asked Rahnab too.

Everybody was happy and wanted to ask something, but Bartholomeu interupted them, "Yes, you'll them meet again . . . and not just with them. We searched the area at the foot of this mountain, and other survivors we have found, those who survived the carnage of Megros City. Women, men, and children. There are not so many, but the important thing is that they have been rescued from the claws of death. Some marnasitis are among them too. They escaped, and they took this way toward this mountain and joined that group. Our Lord helped them and guided them to this place."

"Do you know how many they are?" asked Emos.

"Or who are those who have escaped?" asked Bily . . .

"Is there someone named Galeth among them?" asked Hingus.

Galeth was the older brother of Hingus, who sent his familly to Amnus, but he remained in Megros to fight against Voron's army, trying to save the city.

"I know nothing of these. I just know that by now they should be on Nesus Plateau."

"Let's go and meet them," said some of the heroes. They were even happier upon hearing such news. These small victories increased their courage, their hope, and their belief in the Lord of Light.

"Let's go," said Bartholomeu. "Let's go to Nesus." And everyone prepared for the journey.

The group began to move. The hamaans who lost their birds and our heroes were moving on their feet in a pleasant walk. Only Rahnab, being a child, had the opportunity to go toward that plateau in flight. And, of course, Shigash, because he was quite seriously injured. He was transported on the back of such bird, in some kind of stretcher.

So he can be treated as quickly as possible, some birds that transported Shigash headed with full speed to Nesus. The other birds remained with those who were walking on their feet. Together with those who possessed them, they flew in circles in the air and watched their friends, who were down. Now there was no danger near them, but just in case, they searched the entire surrounding area.

"By sunset we will arrive at our location, and you will be able to see your families," said one hamaan from the group.

All were glad upon hearing this, because they were tired and they wanted to see the ones they love.

It was dark outside. That huge plateau looked tiny because of that sea of banits, marnasits, and hamaans; it was full of tents placed side by side. There were also animals: large animals, small animals in cages, little birds, free big birds. You could also see some sort of a cow or bull, a huge animal used to carry big carts filled with food, objects, women, and children in that long journey.

Even though it was evening, when the group of heroes and hamaans reached the plateau, lots of banits and marnasits were standing outside around the fires that lit the plateau like it was day.

Women were preparing dinner at these fires, children were playing and running carefree, and men were sitting in groups near those fires and talking about what happened and what will be in future.

There were also some places where the women left their cooking and started to cry because her husband, son, or boyfriend had returned alive to them. But there were only few places like these. Few of them survived the slaughter.

When the hamaans and the heroes came near the first tents, the silence was replaced by bustle and noise. More and more people came to salute the group of heroes and hamaans. There was more and more agitation around the tents.

After a while, the elders appeared to salute the group and the hamaans that found them. Efreu, Shigash, and the other leaders of banits, marnasits, and hamaans went toward a huge tent, where they'll stay to discuss what they had to do next.

Emos, Hingus, Billy, and Rahnab went to see their families. Emos went to look after Adela because she was her only family for now. Actually she was not yet, but probably she will be in the near future.

He knew that those missing had returned. But it could be and those who survived the attack in the city Megre. Who knew how many survived in that slaughter? The thought that her father would return could not help her in any way. She knew her father would have given his life to save another. To save one of his fellows.

Adela was waiting for her lover. And for her father. She heard that some banits survived that battle from city of Megres. She hoped that they will return. At first she thought she had lost her father forever. And now it's almost the same, but she still hoped that she will see him again. Half of her heart felt that she was not going to see her father again, but half of her heart hoped.

She was staying near the fire. Her mother prepared something for eat. Only the two of them were near that fire. But Emos will be there soon. Even if she also knew that some of the banits died while they fought with Lord-knows-what creatures, she knew that Emos was a great warrior. And Lord also took care of him every time. So she knew that her lover will come.

"Adela," she heard her mother's voice. The mother awoke Adela from the myriad of her thoughts.

"What is it, Mother?" replied the girl. "You need help?"

"Somebody came to see you," she said. And Emos appeared in front of Adela.

"Emos!" yelled the girl. She turned and quickly ran toward him. Then she kissed and embraced with from all her heart.

"I love you," she said to him. Then she asked him with a smile on her face, "How much do you love me?"

Emos said nothing. He raised his right hand and showed the girl how much he loved her. He used to show her a small distance between his forefinger and thumb. And he used to say that he loved her only that much.

But Adela knew that Emos was just joking. She knew that he loved her more than anything. So she didn't get mad when she saw that little distance between Emos's fingers.

Adela's mother was happier when she saw that someone came to them. Someone that could be lost in all these battles because many young ones lost their lives since those battles against the evil began.

She became happier when she saw that Billy, Hingus, and Rahnab, along with other friends of Emos, came to see them. She invited the young ones to eat with them, and they accepted.

"We need the last key to enter Amnus," began Efreu.

The wise man was staying in front of those who took part of that meeting. The castle where they had stopped was the haaman's home for almost a thousand winters.

The one who seemed to know everything was Vanuh, one of the nineteen kings:

"Yes, we know," said Vanuh.

Vanuh was the leader of hamaans. He was the most respected in these regions. Actually all nineteen kings were, and the banits and marnasits must respect them too. Only those banits from the council of elders, some marnasits, and some hamaans had the privilege to take part of this meeting.

"We all saw that the lizards aren't our allies. Surely we'll see them in the next future, as our enemies," said Efreu.

"And other creatures, also reptiles like these archers," said another one of the nineteen kings.

"I said that we must smash these reptiles before they get reinforcement from the Army of the Dead," said one of the banits' leaders.

"We can't," another king said. Some of my winged saw that the Army of the Dead is closer than ever . . . closer than we think. Maybe we'll have time to smash the reptiles, but we won't have enough time to reach to Amnus castle. And we will be lost forever . . . . all of us.

"Why don't we fight from here against those armies? It's a great castle with great walls. I think we can beat Voron's armies from here."

"You do not understand the force of Voron's armies. He destroyed more tribes bigger than yours, more than ten times bigger," said Vanuh.

Nobody said anything else. They were frightened.

"First thing in the morning is to leave this castle. And take the Amnus way," said Vanuh.

"And for that, we have a lot of work to do," completed Efreu.

So many people were going toward Amnus, known as the city of the Lord. In that group were hamaans flying on their birds and marnasits riding their huge bulls, probably only the leaders. Also there were many hamaans, banits, and marnasits walking. There were lots of people like a huge army. If they stayed in the hamaan's castle they could fight against any army, even against one hundred thousand enemies, but they didn't stay there because the hamaans said so. What do they know that the others don't? And what kind of army will attack them? What kind of creatures will attack them?

"Can I ride one of these creatures?" asked Rahnab to his mother. "Can I?".

His mother looked at Billy. Even if they fought for the same thing, many of the banits were still afraid of these marnasits. They were afraid of those bulls some of the marnasits were riding; they were afraid of those enormous birds. The banits were afraid of any creature because they were smaller than almost any creature from Mania.

But Billy, after seeing how the marnasits were fighting for his brother, now was their best friend. He looked at Marnuk, and the giant made a sign with his head that he will be happy to take the boy. So Billy took his brother and put him one of these huge cattle. And the young boy was so happy, as happy as he was when he flew on that bird.

So our huge group now was going to Amnus. Amnus, the greatest castle city from this planet, was going to be the place where Voron's and Lord of Light's armies will fight for the last time.

The only way to reach Amnus was to climb that mountain, to reach the top of it.

After some long days of cold weather and powerful winds, the group almost reached the top of the mountain. All of them, less the hamaans who wore clothes made by the marnasits, were dressed with thick clothes. They were not so beautiful clothes, but at least they kept them warm. All of them were made from the skin of the creatures killed by the marnasits.

The clothes were sewn with some long and thin pieces of skin. And it looked like these were unfinished.

Now they climbed the mountain walking around him. It was a hard way. From the heat at the foot of the mountain, now they had to face this strong winter. But they had these ugly warm clothes.

Suddenly they reached one crossroad. They could take the right or the left.

The hamaans knew the way they had to choose to reach the Amnus City. But those who were at the front of the group must wait before they would know the right one.

Finally Vanuh reached the crossroad with some of his men and said to the group, at least to those who were near him:

"This is the right way," said Vanuh, showing the road going to the left.

"You heard him, people. We must take to the left," yelled Efreu to the group. "Let's continue our journey!".

"Wait," said Vanuh. "Some of us must choose the right way before reaching Amnus."

Efreu looked at him a little scared. And then he asked him, "Why? And who are those that should do that?"

Without looking at him, Vanuh said to the old man, "Those who took part of the queen's murder."

Billy, Hingus, and the other heroes were near Efreu and Vanuh. They heard about what they were talking about, so they came to hear more of their discussion. "We are ready to face whatever we have to fight with!" said Billy who now had such confidence in their strength.

"My spear is ready to kill any beast!" yelled Hingus.

"Where is Emos?" asked Efreu to the two young ones.

"I am right here, master Efreu," said a voice. Emos was with her fiancée. He kissed her; he looked into her eyes, and without saying anything, he bid her farewell.

"We ready go," said Shigash when the marnasit who went after Marnuk came back with him.

"Yes, let's go," said Efreu.

And the heroes began to walk.

"Wait," said Vanuh. "We need that little boy too."

Once again, Hingus and Emos looked at Billy. The first time the giant had heard that Rahnab must go with them, he was so irritated. But now, after he saw that everyone took care of the boy, he didn't say anything.

He called for Rahnab. The boy came in a hurry when he heard the voice of his brother.

"We are ready to go," said Billy while he was grabbing the little brother by his arms and putting him on one of his shoulders. And he began to walk toward the right way.

The others followed them. Vanuh chose some of his men to follow them. There were almost thirty hamaans, and twenty-five of them took with them those huge birds.

After he talked with the other hamaans, some of those who will remain with the big group, Vanuh followed the heroes, being escorted by five hamaans.

"This is the ice creature's cave. We need to get from them the last key to open the Amnus gate," said Vanuh to his companions.

"So there is the last key," said Hingus to his friends Emos and Billy.

"And perhaps we can convince them to follow us in this war against Voron," completed Vanuh.

"What kind of creature is this cave creature?" asked Rahnab.

Not many of them saw such creatures. But Efreu could answer the boy's question, "Those are friendly creatures if you know how to discuss with them," said Efreu.

"Like those lizards at the beginning," intervened Hingus.

But none of the heroes said anything else. They entered into the cave. It was a huge cave, and everywhere it was ice. Huge icicles were everywhere: on the cave's ceiling, on the cave's floor. If one icicle from the ceiling dropped on our heroes, easily it could kill some of them.

They entered deeper and deeper into that cave. And even so, there was so much light into this cave. The ice reflected the sunlight, which came down through some kind of pipes made by water flow—or by someone probably.

"It's so beautiful!" yelled Rahnab. Since they started the journey, this little boy was always so amazed about everything he saw. When he first entered in that forest where they fought with that creature, he was more than amazed and happy, at least at the beginning, before they had to fight with those creatures. And then when he first saw that white substance, that snow, on the grounds he was also so amazed. He felt the same thing when he saw this cave filled with ice, with so many colors on the walls because of the minerals in them. You can see through the ice in some places, and you saw these colors of minerals. And combined with sunlight and the sun's reflection, it was a very beautiful view—like a beautiful dream.

But wherever there is such a beautiful view, there has to be something that destroys your happiness. A roar of some kind of unknown creature penetrated the silence of that cave. And you cannot find the direction from where the sound came. The echo of that roar went through that cave, and because of so many corridors, now the sound of the roars came from everywhere.

"Dissipate yourself," said Vanuh.

All the members of the group dissipated. Some of the hamaans, Emos and Hingus went straight toward those roars. Rahnab was ready to follow them, but a powerful hand caught him by one of the shoulders and didn't let him to follow the warriors. It was Billy.

The giant looked at him and said with a low voice, "Not so fast. We'll stay here to watch their back."

The real reason was to protect the boy. His life was too much put in danger. Marnuk and some hamaans remained with them. Who knows what else could attack them? The boy was the most vulnerable?

Finally there was a huge creature, as big as that cssilias but with white fur. And he could speak because Vanuh could speak with him in some language the banits never heard of.

"He said that the time has not come," said Vanuh to the others to understand what they were speaking about.

Hingus asked Vanuh, "It's not time for what?"

"They said it's not time for giving us that artifact, the third key of Amnus's gate, because their prophecy didn't come true."

"I'm tired of these prophecies," said Hingus. "Everyone has a prophecy to be fulfilled. First those lizards, now these white cssilias."

The creature said something else to Vanuh.

"What did he say?" asked Hingus again.

Vanuh became upset this time; he didn't say anything else, but you can see on his face that he was upset.

:He said that we need to let this boy who came with us to go with them." And he looked at Billy and Rahnab.

The giant Billy heard what Vanuh had said. He didn't say anything. But it's obvious that he won't give his brother to that creature.

"Not this time," said Hingus.

"Not this time," said Emos. And at the same time the others also said, "Not this time" or "We won't let this happen." Some of them put their hand on their weapons.

"Don't grab your arms," said Vanuh. "He is not alone."

And when he said that, the heroes saw some shadows in the corners of those corridors, which they didn't observe until now.

"They are too much strong to fight with them. We can lose many lives. And they asked us to take the boy only for a few minutes," spoke Vanuh.

"Only if I can go with him," said Billy to them.

Vanuh told something to that creature, and the creature approved something. So Vanuh told to Billy, "He agrees with that."

Emos looked at his friends. That creature could kill him. He looked then to Efreu, but when he saw that the old man was so calm, he didn't say anything else.

So Billy and Rahnab followed the huge creature. With them some other creatures like these white cssilias disappeared.

Actually their shadows distempered because none of our heroes could see them. They were hiding too well to find them. Only the best hunters, like our heroes, could tell that they were watched by something.

The creature began to speak with these words, "I am Kalus. Our Lord chooses you to save this planet. You can see on these walls a prophecy that speaks about you. You can see there a little boy whose work is to find the keys of the Lord's castle. We have the last key, which we are going to give to you. But you should know that you are the only one who can open the great gate. You should tell this to Vanuh so he knows that they have to protect you."

The boy said nothing.

"We can't help you against this war. Vanuh probably wants us to fight with you against the Army of Death. Our only duty was to protect this artifact, the third key for opening the great gate."

"What will happen to you?" asked Rahnab.

When his brother spoke, Billy flinched. He asked his brother, "What?"

But Rahnab didn't answer his brother because the creature continued, "We are not from this world. And it is too soon to speak about this, but we will meet again. This is the way you must go to find the key. Take your brother and go there. Then you have to go straight to the great city Amnus."

After he spoke, the creature left. Rahnab said to his brother, Billy, "Kalus said we must go there."

Billy was taken aback when he heard these words, "Who is Kalup?" he asked.

"It's not Kalup. Kalus. It is his name, that creature I spoke with. He said we must go there to find the key."

Billy said nothing. He didn't hear anything. He put his huge arm on the boy's shoulder, and he said, "Let's go and find that artifact."

And the boys went on that corridor, and after some minutes they found that key. The key was on an ice pedestal. They took the object and went to find the others.

On their way, Rahnab tried to say to his brother that Kalus said they were from the other world, but Billy only listened to his brother without saying anything. "Surely Rahnab is tired because of this journey." He didn't hear anything from that dialogue between Rahnab and Kalus, so he thought it was the boy's imagination.

"It's so great! I never saw anything so big! It's huge this castle!" said one of the elders.

And you can see on all the faces that it was something none had never imagined to see.

"This is Amnus!" said Vanuh. "This is the place where our Lord wants us to stay and fight against His enemies—our enemies."

It was a great city. A city that none could ever built. Only someone like the Lord of Light. The castle was built in steps. The first level was the biggest level with walls more than a hundred meters in height. It was so huge in circumference that fifty, a hundred, maybe even more castles like the one where the hamaans lived could be placed in it and still had remaining space.

If you went higher and higher toward the top of the castle, toward the top levels of the city, you can observe that the castle became thinner. But it also had enough space to put the entire group inside that level of the fortress.

But the group of marnasits, banits, and hamaans didn't know that yet because from where they were, they couldn't see the top of the castles. The city was also higher than a great mountain.

"And this is the place where we must put the three keys."

"Let's put them where they should be put," said one of the elders. "Take one of those artifacts and put it right in the place specially made for it. It is easy to see where you have to put it."

"Wait!" yelled Vanuh. "You shouldn't—"

But he didn't finish his words, and a powerful lightning sent the elder down. Some members from his family tried to help him, but they were very cautious when they had to help him.

"What was that?" asked the injured man's wife.

"We should think before we make any move," said Vanuh.

Then he assured that the injured man was going to live. It wasn't so bad. The injured got up on his feet; he was a little confused, but he was fine.

"There is a riddle," said Vanuh. "It says that only a pure soul with bloody hands could open that gate," spoke Vanuh.

"But this could not be true," said one of the elders.

"Yes, a man couldn't be pure if he killed someone! The laws said that one of the commands says that it's forbidden to kill! A killer can't have a pure soul! So we can't complete this request," said an old man from the group.

Vanuh said nothing. He looked at the gate. He looked at the riddle that was engraved on the stone gate. This huge stone gate was the last thing that stayed on their way; if they won't succeed to open the gate, they surely will die.

Efreu said to Vanuh, "A pure soul is a child. But someone who has bloody hands should be a young boy who fought against Voron's soldiers. We should call such a boy."

So they called for the boys who fought in Megros castle. These boys succeeded to kill some soldiers from the evil force, so it had to be one of them who should open the gate.

Vanuh called for one such boy, and he came. They showed him what to do, but when that boy tried to put that artifact in the right place, the lightning sent him on the ground. And this time the lightning was more powerful than the first.

There was such pressing silence. Nobody spoke. Everyone tried to find a solution. The elders asked the boy if he really killed at least one soldier from Voron's army. They grabbed him by his clothes and asked him if what he said was true. Probably if Efreu didn't intervene to protect him, they surely would beat up the seriously injured boy.

But Efreu stopped them. He knew it's not his fault. Someone who killed any creature couldn't be a pure soul.

More and more people came near the gate. And finally Emose and his friends arrived at the gate. They asked the people around the gate what the problem was and why they didn't enter into the castle. They received the answer from a lady.

When the little Rahnab heard what they didn't succeed to do, he said, "That creature said that I'm the only one who could open the gate."

Everyone started to laugh when they heard the boy. It was a desperate laugh, but even so it was kind of funny to hear that.

Billy grabbed his brother by his shoulders; he raised him in the air, and he tried to leave from there passing through the crowd.

But someone stopped him.

"Wait, Billy! Put your brother down and bring him to me!" said a voice. It was Efreu.

They needed to find any clue that could help them to open the gate. It was their last chance.

The two boys came. Efreu looked at Rahnab and asked him, "Who said those words to you?"

"That huge creature. Billy can say that is true."

"I heard nothing," said the giant. "And it's not the time to say such lies," said the older brother, Billy.

"But this is the truth. I spoke with him."

"Rahnab!" yelled Billy. "It's enough."

"But—"

The boy didn't finish his words, and Billy grabbed him by his shoulders, raised him in the air, and looked at him with such anger that Rahnab didn't say anything more.

"Leave the boy down," said Efreu once again. And after the boy was put down, Efreu began to put his hand on his shoulder and said to him, "Tell me what that creature said to you."

"He said that I'm the only one who could open the gate."

Efreu said nothing. He looked at the gate. It was such a huge gate. Only a huge mechanism could open such.

"It's a strong gate. None could easily destroy such gate," whispered Efreu . . .

"Did you say anything, wise Efreu?" asked Billy. "Do you want me to teach my brother not to lie anymore?"

"Leave the boy alone," said Efreu.

He stopped a moment, and then he continued, "The riddle says that only a pure soul with bloody hands could open that gate. Your soul is pure Rahnab, but you killed that lizard queen so your hands are bathed with blood. So if there is anyone that can open this gate, then you are the one. So open it!"

Rahnab got closer to that gate. He took one of those talismans and prepared himself to put it where it belonged.

It was so quiet. All the people saw what had happened with the others. They were all scared. One by one the boy put the three talismans on their places, and the puzzle was done.

Something divine came down from the sky, a light or something; and when it reached the gate of Amnus, the light dissipated all over the castle. Everywhere on the walls it spread, and then it went higher toward the top of the huge castle. And then it disappeared.

A beautiful sound of harps can be heard everywhere in the city after this light disappeared. A warm sound, a sound that made you feel safe. The torches all over the place lit up at the same time, with blue flames burning.

"This is the divine sound," said Varnuh. "Our ancestors said that the angels sing these songs. And their songs are so powerful that they can destroy any evil enemy. Hearing these songs is the best thing that could happen to us! We are saved! The boy saved us!" yelled Varnuh while he raised his arms in the air as a sign of victory. "We are saved!"

And when the people saw that the gate was opening, they also raised their arms in the air and showed their happiness and their gratitude for their Lord.

Some of them also showed their gratitude for the boy. They took the boy on their shoulders and began to walk with him between the crowds to thank him.

So the gate finally opened. And the people began to enter inside the great city.

All over the corridors you can hear this warm sound of harps. And the torches spread a blue light on these corridors, on the walls—everywhere.

Rahnab and some of his friends ran on these corridors. They entered chamber after chamber. Everywhere they entered they saw so many interesting things.

They saw huge statues describing fights between some huge creatures. Some of them looked like them, but they were huge, and they had huge wings. Some of them were also huge, but they were ugly creatures.

Other chambers were filled with shields, armors, and weapons. Those weapons also radiated a warm and blue light. But none of them had the courage to touch these objects.

There were also lots of chambers where the banits and marnasits could sleep. Hundreds of these kinds of chambers. The elders showed the people where to go. So everyone spread where they were sent. In a few hours all the people settled down in one of those chambers.

In this castle you can also see huge chambers where a huge group of people could pray to the Lord of Light. These praying chambers, unlike the other rooms, had walls made only by glass with huge paintings. On one of the walls, there was a painting depicting seven huge creatures with huge wings, having in their arms huge swords. They were standing like they were put there to protect the one who was praying in that chamber.

"These are angels," said one of the hamaans to those who were looking at these huge glass walls, "the army of the Creator."

Other chambers had painting showing fights between good and evil, fights where the good always won.

There was also a special chamber where only the hamaans could enter.

Rahnab, Efreu, Emos, and the rest of our heroes pointed toward this room. Besides Efreu, who entered into that room when they reached Amnus, the others only heard about this chamber.

"What is this chamber?" asked Rahnab.

"On the walls of this chamber is described the future of this planet, our future," answered Efreu. "It is what it will happen on your planet in the next future."

They reached at the door of that chamber. "Actually it was not a door; it was some kind of field that kept the banits and the marnasits outside." Efreu entered in that room through that field, but when Hingus also tried to go through it, he couldn't. For them this field was like a wall. It was a light blue wall, the same light blue that was everywhere. And they also couldn't see anything from the other side of the wall. But the hamaans could see them.

"We all saw the signs," said Varnuh to the others. "We all try to help the 'white horse' to win the battle against evil . . . against Voron. But the 'white horse' won few battles against evil. Not so many people choose to fight against Voron. More of them choose to fight against us by his side. We saw how many banits and marnasits came into Amnus. More of them were touched by evil's hand, and now they are his army."

He took a short break and then he continued, "And now the 'red horse' was sent on this planet, and a great war between our Lord's army and against Army of Death will be born. And they are many times more than our army. We also knew that the generals of Voron's armies were released from their prisons, and they are waiting for their master to tell them when the moment to attack us has come. Probably they are right now at the gate of Amnus, waiting for their armies to reach at the gate."

He took another break, and then he said again, "We also know that some of the rest of the seals were broken. We saw that the angel of our Lord took the scepter and filled it with fire from the divine altar and hurled it down over Mania. So thunders and voices, lightnings, and earthquakes started to hit our planet. Mountains in lames came down over us. Stars burning like a torch came over us. And since then, there are only some places on this planet where you can find forests and living beings. And because of these mountains in flames, because of these burning stars during our ancestors' time, there was no water on the surface of the planet. Our seas became blood, and then it disappeared for good. Now there are some huge rivers that originate from the inside of the planet."

He stopped once again. He looked at the crowd of hamaans, and he continued, but this time he was sadder then ever, "Now we all know that when the fourth angel will sing, that means the great war has begun. The dark age will begin. It will be darker than ever; there will not be day and night, morning and evening. Only few stars will light every time, and and we won't see the moon anymore. And we should show more fear because of the other voices of the trumpet of the three angels who are ready to blow! When the fifth angel will sound, a star will fall from heaven to earth, giving the key to open the deep fountain. The sun and sky will be darkened by the smoke pit.

And from the smoke will come creatures upon the earth, and they will have great And in those days, men will seek death, and they'll want to die, but death will flee from them. The next angel will also bring a great course on us. He will release the four angels. They will be the captains of the armies. And one of them will be the captain of the horses and those who sat on them. And the horses will have breastplates of fire and brimstone Iachint, and from their mouths will come fire and smoke and brimstone.

"And for the last, when the seventh angel will speak, the will of our Lord will be done."

Everyone listened what Varnuh was saying. They all knew that what the future reserved for them was not so easy. But they had to prepare for whatever they had to fight against.

Varnuh wanted to continue his speech, but someone from the crowd disturbed him.

"Look! The battle of Mania begins now."

I don't know if the battle has begun now, but on the walls of that chambers, you can see that the walls transformed into some sculptures. And many battles were described now on these walls. Some of the things that had happened were written on that sculptures, but what is going to happen only appears now."

"Yes, it's true," said Varnuh. "I fear that we don't have as much time as I thought to prepare against Voron's army. So we must go now and prepare the banits and the marnasits for the battle. Each one of you should take a group of marnasits and banits and lead them. So go! Prepare them against this Army of Death."

And the hamaans began to leave that chamber. And you can see all these hamaans going through the wall and toward the chambers where the marnasits and banits were sleeping. They must be prepared for whenever the Army of Death will reach the gate of Amnus.

But maybe they are at the gates right now. Who knows?

"What happened?" asked some of the people from the crowd.

"I'm not sure," answered the others. "But I think that Efreu and Varnuh are discussing with an angel."

"You should take these weapons if you want to fight against the evil army. But you should know that you can use the power of these weapons only inside. If you get outside with them, their powers will be lost."

The one who spoke was Michel, the angel sent over by the Lord of the Light to help the people of this planet called Mania.

"But it won't be easier to help us fight against evil," asked Efreu.

"This is the will of our Lord. We can't help you," said the angel. "It's your battle."

"But the evil will use so many ways to destroy us. So many forces, and we will be lost if we will have to face it," said Varnuh.

But Michael said only one thing before he disappeared, "Your faith will save you!" And a light blue cloud came around him. After that the light blue cloud dissipated into the air.

Thousands of soldiers prepared in the city of Amnus, ready to fight against the Army of Death. Almost all the women, children, and old people were now on the upper floors of the castle. The others, those who were prepared to fight against Voron—men, women, young ones, and even some not-so-old people—sat on the walls of the first level of the city.

And from there you can see a sea of soldiers: the Army of Death. And none of us ever saw such ugly and terrifying creatures. You can see dead soldiers, some of them almost without flesh on them; they were bones and putrid flesh and skin. You can also see some creatures looking like some very huge lions, with huge wings and with something looking like the top of spear at the head of their tails.

And there were also lots of other creatures like some kind of horsemen, but theirs horses were in flames—black horses with fire in their eyes and on their mane and with a huge fire cornucopia where their nose should be. And if those were already terrifying creatures, you should wait for their masters. Those who were sitting on these horses were huge, even more than a marnasit, with very huge spears and shields, wearing huge and strong armors and helmets. You can see only their flaming eyes.

There were also those creatures that were ten times taller than a marnasit, those who distroyed the walls of Megros castle and helped the Death Army to conquer Megros. Some huge creatures with many heads, like the creature which attacked our heroes into that forest were they killed the cssilias.

Each hamaan spoke to his group of men, trying to tell them about the attackers, before the fight will begin.

"You should be careful with those winged. The top of their tail is poisonous."

"You should be careful not only of their tails. Everything in this army, every weapon, is poison. Their arrows, their swords, their breath."

"Watch your back when you see the shadows. These creatures were born long, long time ago. They were buried since then into their prisons, but now they escaped from those prisons. Voron helped them, so they are his servants now. So you should watch for them because you'll never know from where they can appear."

And somwhere into that darkness, which fell over the entire planet, were thousands and thousands of creatures. And who knows what abomination could rise from that dark?

But you shouldn't think that those creatures wer doing nothing while the hamaans spoke to the others. The castle was attacked on the north side by hundreds of these creatures. Those lions were the first creatures that tried to attack the castle. They had on their back csillias wearing armors and with huge weapons. I said they were the first who tried to attack the castle because even they made lots of damages between the castle's army, their lost was bigger.

Many banits fired with bolts from the crosbows, which they found in Amnus. And those bolts were blessed by the Lord of Light. More than a hundred of banits shouted against each winged lion. And so many bolts killed every target.

"Kill the manticores. Kill the lions!" yelled the captains.

And even if it was very hard to shoot against those lions, the castle's army succeeded to chase away the lions.

Some of the lions also succeeded in killing many banits. Using their jaws, teeth, and tails, those creatures were great soldiers. And those who sat on them also were great soldiers. One csillias could kill twenty banits with their huge weapon. So the banits and marnasits lost lots of men too.

But the huge problem from Voron's army was those skeletons. Thousands of those skeletons climbed on the walls without any problems, using only their hands and legs. They were so quick that the defenders had to retreat more and more. And because those skeletons came from everywhere, the defenders were split into little armies. And this was not good because they were easy to defeat.

But this was their strategy: splitting in pieces the defenders.

When a group of men was almost detached from the others, some hamaans helped the group by using lightnings, fire waves, and many other weapons they were gifted with.

So the banits, marnasits, and hamaans did more damage to Voron's army than the Army of Death did to them. And this was a good thing, but the disadvantage was that Voron's army was many times larger than their enemies.

"We won this battle," said one of the elders. "And now the time has come, the time to finally destroy our enemies."

The skeletons retreated. The other creatures did the same.

"Let's distroy our enemies!" said the other elders.

"Our Lord said through his angel's word to us: do not get out of Amnus because the power that He gave us won't follow us outside the Amnus gate," said Efreu to them.

"We won't need His power anymore. You see what we succeeded with our own hands. He helped us by giving us a place where we can protect our families, weapons to fight, but now it's time for us to destroy the evil once and for all."

Many banit soldiers, thousands of them, seeing that they were facing the power of Voron's army, wanted to fight more than ever. It's like greed: the more you have, the more you want.

In their case, the warrior's blood began to flow through their veins. The thirst of victory made them so noisy, so ablazed.

"Don't take this way! Remember our Lord's words!" Efreu tried to tell them. But his voice couldn't cover the voice of thousands of men.

And without saying or waiting anything, hundreds of them prepared their weapon to get out and attack their enemies.

Hundreds of spears went outside the gates. Some of the elders were the captains of this attack against Voron's army.

Hundreds of men were prepared to fight against the Army of Death with their swords. These swordmen were entirely strong armored. You could see only theirs eyes you could see.

Somewhere outside Amnus gates, the Army of Death tried to regroup. When you see the chaos that disorganizes the army, you surely think that this is the oportunity to destroy them.

So the banits began the attack against enemies. The spearmen were in front with their spears. Anyone who was in their way could be. So the lines of the enemies were restricted more and more. The sahtaris were quickly moving backward.

But after a while the sahtaris didn't move so quickly. When the group of sahtaris became bigger, thousands of them and other creatures from the Army of Death, the enemies prepared to answer the attack from the banits.

When the banits saw that the Army of Death wanted to fight, the spearmen stopped, and the swordsmen with hard armors came from the back.

And in few seconds the disaster came over Voron's army. The banits went through the sahtaris without big efforts. The bones and the heads of those skeletal bodies were everywhere. In few words, it looked like the banits were going to win this war easily; even the huge creatures were running away.

After the banits smashed two to three thousand of sahtaris, the swordsmen stopped. They stopped because they saw some sahtaris riding some creatures. But these sahtaris, hundreds of them, were wearing strong armors like banits' swordsmen. And their horses were also wearing strong armors. But those horses were not just like horses. The creatures had four legs, hoovers at the end of the legs, a head looking almost like a horse's head. But the difference is that these horses had burning eyes and tails. With red eyes like fire and a tail that was on fire, these creatures frightened the banits, the swordsmen.

The captains sent the swordsmen in the back and called the spearmen to take their places.

"Swordsmen in the back! Spearmen in the front!" yelled the captains.

The spearmen came in front. They took their spears and strutted them into the ground. After that they bended the spears at thirty degrees and waited for the enemy. This was the strategy that any captain could use against a cavalry.

The horses began to move slowly and then quickly and quickly. But the cavalry could be distroyed by those spears, if it's only strategy was to frontally attack the banits.

So the distance between the two armies became smaller: five hundred meters, two hundred meters, one hundred, fifty, and then—

"Those who will not listen to the Word will perish"—this was what happened to the banits.

The evil cavalry, those demons riding other demons, went through the banits' line like a lion through a flock of sheep.

The spears broke like toothpicks into the demons' strong armors. The spears couldn't penetrate both sahtaris' and horses' armors. So the cavalry easily trampled the soldiers from the banits' army. Some men were smashed by the horse's hooves, and some were carried hundreds meters away stuck into the iron awns from the armors. The armors of the horses and the shields of sahtaris had awns on them, so huge that they could penetrate a banit's body. So many spearmen and even strong armored swordsmen were stuck into the iron stakes.

After the cavalry got through the defenders' lines, they reached the walls. So those sahtaris turned back the horses to destoy what remained from those defenders. Even if lots of banit soldiers were gone, hundreds of them were still alive, and the sahtaris wanted to kill them all. And it seemed that nobody could save them.

Almost nobody.

Efreu and the others couldn't stay and watch, so they had to do something.

"Those are the 665 Voron's horsemen, sahtiri-riding nightmares. A cavalry that only an army of angels could destroy," yelled Efreu. "But we must try help our brothers."

Many courageous men went to open the Amnus gates and try to save those who seemed to be lost. But not even Efreu's fireballs could hurt such a horsemen.

It's true that the evil cavalry was a little bit confused because of the other group of people who got out from Amnus castle. It looked like they wanted to attack the other group, but their leader reorganized them. The small group of courageous men didn't convince them to don't attack again the spearmen and swordsmen. The only thing that Efreu and others could do was to give some time to their brothers, to help those who were hurt to get on their feet and try to run away and save their lives. But they were lost because no weapon could harm those horsemen.

Shigash the giant and four of his men were the only people that made some damage into Voron's cavalry. Riding some "ksan," some huge rhino buffalos, with huge horns, each marnasit chose some horsemen to attack. each buffalo had four horns: two were on his pout, like a rhno, and two were on his head, just like the buffalo.

Some horsemen were stung by the rhino buffalos; other shatiris were slammed to the ground. None of the horsmen were killed, because you can't kill a dead creature, but at least Shigash and the others gave some more time to the swordsmen and spearmen. Efreu and the other courageous men fought with those sahtiris that had fallen from their horses, but like I said, the only thing they succeeded to do was to help for a short time the others.

The swordsmen and the spearmen also fought against the horsemen. The diffrence between this attack and other was that it is a "defending attack." Because the soldiers from the evil army couldn't be killed, the only thing that the soldiers from Lord of Light's army could do was to push away the sahtiris and theirs horses with a huge price. All the ksans were dead now. Those huge creatures, three times bigger than the evil horsemen, threw away lots of horsmen, but finally they got killed by the evil army. Other soldiers from the banit army were dead. Some of the group of courageous men were also dead. Two marnasits from the group of five riders were also dead.

But more than two hundred of swordsmen and spearmen, easily or badly injured, were saved.

Those who remained on the Amnus walls and saw the battle opened the gate when they saw their brothers approaching.

The regrouped cavalry chased the survivors, but most of them were saved because after they got inside the gate, the weapons that helped Lord of Light's army to defend Amnus once helped them this time too.

Two horsemen were distroyed by the banits' arrows. The nightmare creatures, the two horses, also transformed into dust after they were touched by the hamaans' fireballs.

So the power of the creatures were with them again. But now Voron's army was more powerfull, bigger than during the beginning. More sahtaris, skeletons, climbed the walls. A sea of those creatures attacked the Amnus castle, and because of their number, the only thing that the defenders could do was to retreat. And they did so.

"What should we do?" asked one of the scared elders. The question was adressed to Vanuh.

"We should have faith," answered Vanuh to the elders.

"But—" the same elder tried to say.

"You did enough!" Vanuh cut his words. "We must repair what was done wrong."

Vanuh had no time to argue or to discuss with anyone. He told Emos and other captains, "Each of you take some men and go on the lower levels and find any survivors. We shouldn't let them alone."

In few seconds, lots of group of twenty to thirty men went to find any survivors. The gate of this level of Amnus opened. On the other side were many skeletons, but the groups of soldiers smashed them quickly. Using those blessed swords, maces, spears, or any other weapon, surounded by that blue light, the banits, hamaans, and marnasits, which had left to save the others, had no problem destroying the soldiers of death. And then, all of them disappeared on the corridors of the lower levels. Let's hope we will see them again.

"Help them," said Emos to some of his men.

His elite soldiers, some of the same age friends which he trained with when on Mania were better times, five or six marnasits, very good and strong warriors and some hamaans, those that almost couldn't be killed by anyone, this group of soldiers smashed the group of skeletons they've met. More than ten men tried to fight against them, but if Emos wouldn't come with his men, they would be lost forever.

"Thanks, our Lord," said some of the men. "Thanks to our saviors."

"We lost so many men," said another from the saved group.

"Let's go down some more," said Emos. "Surely there are more men who are waiting for us to help them."

"NO!" yelled the one who seemed to be the leader of that group. "We can't go there!"

"We must help anyone who could be helped," said one marnasit.

"You can't. We can't," said the men. "They are too strong," said the captain of the saved men.

"We should try," Emos answered back to him.

"We were more than two hundred men. We had many men like you," said the men, adressing the hamaan. "But some kind of creature attacked us. We didn't know where they came from. They appeared from nowhere. And they decimate our little army. We are the only one who survived."

It was a huge chamber, something like a huge library. Many learnings were probably on those objects that looked like ancient books. The thousands of objects were put on shelves made by wood and stone. And many of the shelves were pieced together with the books that were on them.

"It's too much quiet and too much less light in this room," said the hamaan.

Because of the events, it was only now the soldiers noticed that in this chamber the blue light disappeared.

The hamaan saw one of his people. The hamaan was dead. So the captain of the two hundred soldiers didn't lie. The hamaan bent down to look what had happened to the others. He looked very scared at the hamaan who was lying down; then he said to Emos and the others, "Run and don't look back, any of you," said the hamaan.

But he said that so quietly that even if all the men heard him no one of them did or said anything. All the men looked at his frightened face. The hamaan looked at the walls of the chamber they were staying. Everywhere in that chamber was destroyed, and there were many dead banits and hamaans, two or three huge unknown creatures, and hundreds of skeletons.

"This can't be true. Such things shouldn't happen," said the same hamaan quietly.

He looked at the group of men, and he said to them, "We are doomed. Only our Lord can save us now. Run and—"

But he didn't finish his words. Something black stabbed him, and then it disappeared as quickly as he appeared.

The hamaan instantly died. And the others were quickly killed by some shadows.

"Run! Run! You can't fight against these creatures!" yelled the other hamaans from the group.

So everyone tried to escape from the attack. The only way to defend themselves was to run and to try not to be hurt by those shadows. Actually they try not to be killed by them because any injury made by the shadow's weapons was deadly because of the unknown poison.

So everyone from the group was terrified. Everyone jumped, tumbled, and even tried to use their shields to protect themselves. But for some of them, this wasn't enough to save them. Every shield was broken by those powerful shadows.

Emos stopped from time to time to try to help his men, but it was useless. He can't do anything again with those shadows. Maybe their weapons could kill those shadows, but they can't touch them. If anyone tried to stab one shadow, the shadow quickly disappeared before any weapon could hurt it. They weren't fast enough. Not even the hamaans could hurt them.

The group dissipated all over the corridors. Emos, the leader of the group, together with four banits, two hamaans, and one marnasit ran on one of the corridors. And it looked like two shadows followed them.

"Stay togheter. This is the only way, our only a chance to stay alive!" yelled Emos.

They reached one wall at the end of the corridor. Emos didn't lose his temper, and he said to the men, "Owl formation."

Because Emos trained with these warriors and with the entire group in those few days they had to prepare themselves, he taught them some war tactics. Also, being a friend to them, he listened to them for good tactics. So they trained well.

The owl should be realized by more than eight men. But even so, they had to defend themselves, and this tactic seemed to be the best. One man was staying in front of the group. That one was Emos, the one who was most exposed to the attack. The other two stayed on his left and right side; they were the hamaans. The hamaans' role was to protect the left and right side of the group. The marnasit was staying right behind Emos. His giant stature let him see everything in front of him, even Emos before him. And the banits must protect the hamaans. Two of them should protect one hamaan, and the other two should protect the other hamaan.

They were prepared to fight the shadows. But even if they were prepared, they were frightened too after seeing what they had to face.

All the eyes looked everywhere. But they saw nothing. There was almost darkness on that corridor. The hamaans couldn't made light with their scepter as much as they wanted. They can only made light to help the group to see until five meters away. So they couldn't see far as they nedeed. They also didn't hear anything.

"Maybe they have left," whispered one of the banits.

"They don't leave anyone alive; they feed with our souls, so they have to kill us."

"Yes, but I see none of—"

He didn't finish his words. Something hit one hamaan with such power that he broke his scepter, and he was thrown away like a dishcloth. It cracked the huge helmet from the marnasit's head, and it cut one banit's armor like a bread.

The hamaan was down while the banit and the marnasti were dizzy because of the powerful hit.

The attack came from the inside of the group, so the tactic they chose to use to defend themselves was not so good.

"Throw away the things they touched with the weapon," said the hamaan.

The marnasit quickly threw away his helmet, and the banit also quikcly threw away his armor, and this was a good decision because some kind of acid began to burn the metal near the nasty cut made by the shadow's sword. Surely one shadow was the attacker.

The armor and the helmet began to emanate vapors from the toxic gas, from that poison, and the metal was melting in the place where the nasty cuts were made.

"Be careful," said Emos to them. "The attack could repeat in any moment."

And the attack repeated. This time a shadow attacked Emos and the marnasit. The powerful hit of the shadow cut marnasit's mace, made by strong metal, into two pieces, and almost touched Emos. In fact, the first person attacked by the shadow was Emos. The captain felt in some way that he was going to be attacked, and he riposted, avoiding the poisoned weapon and the shadow. A voice of an injured woman, a terrified sound like it was pulled off by a dying person, was heard just near Emos and then somewhere on the corridor.

"You heard it? How could that be possible?" asked the hamaan.

Emos was also amazed. How could that be possible? Did that mean that anyone could hurt these shadows? But the hamaans said they can't do anything against them. So what happened?

They waited for another attack, but nothing happened. You could hear ttheir breath—nothing else . . .

"They're gone," said the marnasit after some moments.

"Yes, I think they left," said one of the hamaans. He looked very surprised at Emos. Who could be this young man? Why did he have the power to hurt the shadows? None of them, none of the hamaans, which were pure souls, could ever hurt any shadow.

"We should find a way to escape," said Emos.

All of them looked everywhere to find a way to take down the wall.

"There has to be some kind of mechanism that should open this wall," said one of the hamaans.

But the marnasit took a huge axe and smashed it into the wall. The wall became pieces, so they can see another corridor between the holes he made. He smashed the axe more easily one more time, and he made a hole so everyone could go through it.

"We should cover the hole, so the shadows couldn't go through it," said a banit.

"It's useless. They can go through walls," answered one hamaan. "So let's go quickly to the upper levels of this city before those shadows come back with backups."

"I think this is the way," said Emos to the group. "We should take this way."

"Listen to our captain," said the hamaans too. "Let's go in that direction."

So the group took it; the more they approached the stairs, the more they could hear the voices of their people.

"I think we're saved," said Emos while he ran with his friends to save their lives.

"What's happening?" asked some of the people who can't see who was speaking in front of the chamber.

"Michael, the angel of our Lord, is speaking with our leaders," said someone from the crowd. "They are at the gate . . . and they are huge."

Now the group of defenders was almost on the top of the castle. At this level the thousands of men, women, and children stayed agglomerated.

They were terrified because of all that happened.

"All these happened because once again Voron trespassed our Lord's command. Those shadows you've tried to fight with are his guards. His strongest fighters. Not as strong as us, but you've seen their power."

Efreu said to Michael, "Our only hope is that our Lord will have mercy for us and send his help. Otherwise, we will all—"

"He already did that. I was sent by Him to stop Voron's will. You should know that."

But Michael was interrupted by a sound. It was the howl of rage of crazy women—the shadows.

"Take care of the women and the children," said Michael to Efreu. "We will take care of those shadows."

And if when he spoke with Efreu, Michael looked like a banit, now he transformed himself. His body began to shine like the sun. Everyone covered their eyes because they could go blind.

The light burned only for few moments; then everything became normal—almost normal.

Everyone who was there saw how Michael grew to more than four times bigger than a marnasit. On his back were two huge wings. He was dressed in a white robe, which almost touched the floor, with red labels and collar. On his head Michael wore a gold crown, the sign of being the angels' captain. His weapon was a huge scepter, and his shield was some kind of a field that surrounded him.

"An angel," said someone to Efreu.

But the wise answered him, "He is not an angel. He is a seraphim."

"What is a seraphim?" asked the same old man.

"The captain of the angels. One of them. There are two of them. The other captain is a heruvim. He is—"

But once again Efreu was interrupted by an incredible apparition. Another huge angel appeared into that huge room. But this angel wore an armor on his body and armored pieces on his legs and arms. Under this armor he also had a white robe but not as long as the seraphim's. His weapon was a huge sword, and the sword was in flames. Actually the sword didn't have a sharp blade. The blade was this fire that took the form of a blade. In his other hand was a huge shield. And everything was shining like gold but much stronger than iron or steel. His helmet also had the same captain sign drafted on it.

"This is the other captain, heruvim . . . Gabriel," said Efreu to the old man. "Nothing, besides our Lord, could kill them when they fight together. Even Voron could be hurt and maybe killed by them," completed Efreu.

The two captains were ready to fight against the shadows. And with them remained our group of heroes and some other brave men to fight all together those creatures.

The howls were becoming closer and closer. Then finally they appeared.

Now everyone could see them because of the light that was around all of them who was fighting on the angels' side. And not only they could see those beasts, but because of the angels' breath, which was throw over all the defenders, the BLESS's breath, all our heroes could now fight against these shadows.

The scepter from Michael' s hand had sent a blue light that burned the shadows. Gabriel with his huge burning sword killed two to three shadows at once. Everyone now had his weapon touched by that blue light, the light of the Creator. The archmen who were there—the hamaans, the marnasits, the banits—all of them can now kill those shadows. All the weapons, all the arrows' top and even the shields, were covered by that blue light. And besides that, if the banits and marnasits could not see the shadows the first time they met them, now all of them can see those creatures. And those creatures didn't have any chance against Gabriel and Michael and against the others.

Moreover, any banit, marnasit, and hamaan touched by the shadow's weapon was cured by Gabriel or by Michael. The Lord of the Light gave them that power.

Finally no shadow appeared. Maybe hundreds of them were destroyed by the angels and our heroes.

"I think that's all," said Michael. "They lost too many of them."

"Yes, but we must be cautious because we don't know what creature can come over us," said Efreu.

"Those are Voron's strongest creatures," answered Gabriel to Efreu and the others. "There is no other creature that could attack us," said the angel. "The truth is that they shouldn't attack you. This is not their war. But once agin Voron did as he likes, and our Lord sent the two of us to repair what was broken."

"Yes," completed Michael. „He sent us to repair everything that was broken. And we repaired everything. This means that the war, your war, ended. And you are those who won the war."

Hearing this, everyone became happy. Some of them tried to contain their happiness but only in the begining. After all, an angel could say only the truth.

In front of the elders and the other leaders, Gabriel and Michael spoke, "Our Lord commanded us to tell you that the war is over. He told Voron that the war on this planet was won by the good side. So the men that had a pure life and remained alive after the battles with Voron's army, those are the men that deserve the legacy of an undying life. And these will happen soon. It will happen sooner than you think but not until the Lord's will is entirely done."

"But will Voron respect our Lord's will?" asked one of the elders.

"Voron has to respect our Creator's will. Otherwise, he could be destroyed by Him."

"Why didn't the Lord destroy Voron until now?" asked another elder.

"Because Voron has his duty," answered Michael. "From the beginning, all the peoples had the right to choose between good and evil. They chose to know good and evil. And if this was their will, it has to be someone to represent the good, Our Lord, and someone to represent evil, and for that is Voron."

"And what if Voron decided to attack us again?" asked Emos. "Can you help us if he attacked us?"

"This wouldn't happen. Our Lord already told him that the war is ending," answered Gabriel. "And if Voron tried to disobey the Lord's will, it will be—"

But Gabriel was interrupted by something. Michael also felt something. The blue light and the calm music that appeared after the shadows were distroyed disappeared once again. But what else can attack them? Voron had no army to send against them. And what could it be that even the angels were afraid? They had never been afraid of something, except the Lord of the Light. Maybe not even Voron could fight against those two captains because once Voron was the first captain of the Lord of Light. Once he was His best warrior. He was still a good warrior, but he had stopped being the Lord's captain. He was his enemy.

"I think he's S'Hamoack," said Michael to Gabriel.

"We can beat him," answered Gabriel.

"Who is Shamac?" asked Emos.

"S'Hamoack, answered Eferu to him, "Voron's son. Voron made him from the Deep Flames Mountain."

"We'll fight on your side against him," said Hingus.

"Yes, we'll help you," said Billy.

"Run away! You have no power against that creature! Only—"

But once again the seraphim didn't finish his words. Two hamaans and three banits became ashes in one second.

"Run! All of you!" yelled Michael when he saw what had happened.

All the men ran away. They didn't even know what attacked them since they didn't see their attacker.

The fight began in that huge chamber. The seraphim and the heruvim were fighting together against some creatures all made by fire. From time to time that creature took a human form, a giant form, bigger even than the two angels. He was throwing fire arrows from everywhere toward the two angels because the fire creature could be in more places at same time. From that human form, he entered into the ground like he was melting, and then he got out from the ground in more places. Fire walls raises in more places and from them were fired fire arrows.

But the angels were very fast. They had time to avoid the attacks. After the fire creature sent that fire storms of arrows against one angel, the angel avoided the fire using his powers and his weapons, and then he attacked the source of the arrows.

When Michael was attacked, he used his scepter every time to create a shield against the fire arrows, and then he sent lightnings against the source of the fire. And every time he did that, the creature yelled because of the pain, and then the fire wall disappeared, only to reappear in another one.

Gabriel protected himself against the fire with his huge shield, moving fast from one corner to the other, or putting the sword against the fire arrows. After he avoided the attack, he hit the creature with the sword, and the creature also yelled because of the pain.

But even if the creature was touched by the angels' weapons so frequently, the fire creature didn't show any sign that it's going to give up the fight.

The fighters were now in some kind of courtyard at the last level of the castle. The courtyard was situated in the middle of the castle. From the avanpost the places from the walls that were in that courtyard, many people could see the great fight between the angels and Voron's son.

Everywhere there was fire—on the walls, in the courtyard, in the castle's chambers—everywhere. The banits, marnasits, and the hamaans from the walls looked terrified at how the fire creature came closer and closer at the chambers where all the women, children, and old people were.

"The creature is trying to reach the children," yelled one of the captains.

And some brave warriors jumped from the walls to help the angels. But they were without any help. When they reached in front of the fire walls and they tried to hurt the creature, their weapons almost had no effect. Even if the weapons were blessed by the Lord of Light, they had no power against Voron's son. And the only thing the brave men did was to die. The creature sensed that it was being attacked by some people, so it burned them in a second.

"Stay away!" yelled Michael. "Or you are all going to die!"

And he continued to follow the flames.

Finally, the angels and S'Hamoack stopped somewhere in the courtyard. Michael and Gabriel stayed in front of the creature. The creature began to add his flames, which were all over the place until that moment, took his real form. It was a huge creature, bigger than an angel. And it was all fire. All his body parts looked like they were made from magma.

Instead of arms, the creature had weapons made by that magma and covered by fire. It could make from that burning magma any weapon he wanted—axe, spear, sword—whatever he wanted.

So the creature was ready to face the angels. It looked at the two angels, who were prepared to fight against S'Hamoack; he roared so powerfully and threw fire breath against the angels. And then, even if it was so huge, it attacked the angels so fast that only such angels like Gabriel and Michael could avoid that.

After the fire roared, the creature attacked both angels at the same time. The creature could extend more than seven to eight meters in length, transforming his hand into a weapon, and he hit with such power that Gabriel's only escape was his special shield.

Such strong magma was the creature's body. When the angels succeeded in hitting the creature with their weapon, it was just like they hit a huge rock—a huge burning rock—and all of us know how unplesant it is when you hit with power a huge rock. It shakes your entire body.

Even if the courtyard where the angels were fighting against that creature was so huge that thousands of banits could stay there, it still seemed like it was to little for them because everywhere was fire. The banits and marnasits ran from place to place, trying to extinguish the fire. Even the angels had some problems with this fire because they had to search for some corners of the courtyard where there was no fire and try to attack the fire creature from there.

Suddenly, after he fought a while with the angels, S'Hamoack left the courtyard. He was searching for something, for someone. Michael and Gabriel followed him.

"Move away! Let him pass!" yelled the angels while they ran on the corridors after the creature.

Even the angels flew after the fire creature as they could hardly chase him.

Finally they stopped somwhere where many people waited for the end of this war. Some of them might think that the end of this war meant to die and to become the servants of the Army of Death, Voron's servants.

Almost all of the rest of the banits, marnasits, and hamaans that survived were there. So if the creature threw fire over them, many or maybe all of them could die.

The creature laughed when he saw that almost everyone was there. The angels were also there, and when they reached that place, they came in front of the fire creature so they can protect the last survivors of Mania.

Suddenly he threw a fire storm against a group of people, but Gabriel blew the fire arrows using his wings. Then the creature sent a meteor shower against another group of children, women, and old people; but Michael stopped it. The stones in flames thrown against the people and the meteor shower were stooped by some kind of field.

The creature laughed once again. Everything was a game for him. He knew that the angels can't afford to attack him again because if the fire creature dissipated his fire again, like he did when he fought with the angels, many people could die. So it's better for the heruvim and seraphim to stay with their eyes on S'Hamoack, so they can help the people from the attacks.

Once again suddenly the creature disappeared, but this time even everyone was more scared than ever; the creature didn't show his body anywhere. Even the angels were a little bit scared, not for themselves but for the people, for the rest of what had reamained.

"Where could it be?" asked Gabriel looking at Michael. "What plans does it have?"

"I don't know," answered Michael to the other captain of the angels. "I don't know."

Efreu, Emos, Shigash, and other heroes came near the huge angels.

"Where could it be?" asked Emos.

"We don't know," answered Michael. "But surely he is here somewhere."

Shigash spoke to them, "Me heared noise there."

But everyone heard that noise as well.

"Stay here!" said Gabriel to the others. "Go to the others and wait for us there."

And the two angels went toward the place where the noise was heard. And this was their mistake.

The creature, like any evil from this universe, had a strategy. It looked like he wants to kill our group of heroes as they, with some other hamaans, marnasits, and banits, were now sourounded by a fire wall circle.

Michael and Gabriel felt that something was wrong before they reached the place where the noise and a huge fire began, so they returned quickly to the group of men, but it was too late. Who knows if they can help the poor men?

But still they began to attack the fire wall because they knew that it was the creature's body. Michael threw his spells against that creature, and Gabriel used his swords and his shield to hurt the creature. Even if the fire creature was seriously injured by the two angels, it didn't let any of the men escape.

The hamaans used their scepters to protect the group, the banits and the marnasits used their shields, and the angels hit the creature again and again and again.

But even so, the creature resisted against the attacks. The men's shields began to melt, so they had to throw them, the hamaans' fields made by their scepter began to become smaller and smaller they almost smashed the group of people. Only the angel's attacks were more and more powerful. And this was the reason that made the fire creature to give up in attacking the heroes. With one last groan of pain, the creature totally disappeared. His melting body slowly dissolved, and then what remained were only huge steamy rocks. The fire completley disappeared.

The heroes were now standing on their legs. The banits and the marnasits thanked the hamaans for their huge effort. If they didn't use their power together, all of them could die in a second, and then all of them thanked the angels. Without them they surely were gone forever.

"I think it's dead," said Emos while he extinguished the fire from his arms. Yes, from his arms because the powerful fire burned parts of his armors and his skins. And he wasn't the only one with wounds. Some of the others were also burned on their hands, on their legs, and on their faces. Even the hansome Hingus was burned on his hands and on his face. A serious wound. His hair was burned entirely in some places. You can see the skin of his head.

The marnasits' armors, those powerful skins that protected them from sharp blades and arrows, were also burned in some places. And their bodies were also injured.

But the most important thing was that everyone was alive. None of the heroes died.

"Yes, I think he is dead," said Gabriel after a while. The two angels waited for a while to see if they could sense anything coming from that creature; it was only later they assured the others that the creature was dead.

"Yes," said Michael, "S'Hamoack, the son of Voron, must be dead. This is a victory that none of you could expect. Not even us, the angels, could expect such a thing."

The other group of people came to see if they can help their heroes in taking care of their wounds.

With these two angels sent by the Lord to help them, for the first time over the last weeks, the people of Mania, or what remained of them, felt safe. They can rest without any concern because they saw the power of the seraphim and heruvim. And nothing can beat them in a fight, not even Voron's son, maybe not even Voron, the one that was once an angel. Not even his power could beat these two angels.

The angels were now the sentinels of those people. Meanwhile, some of them asked the angels, "What is going to happen with us now?"

"The evil is destroyed. Voron surely understands that he has no more power against you. Now that his son is dead and his troops ran away, the only thing that remains is to wait to become our Lord's servants. Just like the hamaans are. And since then fighting against Voron and his armies and helping other people from other planets will be your own pourpose."

"This means that Voron wasn't defeated once and for all."

"No," said the Gabriel. He smiled. "This is one of the many battles between our Lord and Voron. And our Lord won this battle."

"This is a good thing," said another person.

"Yes, indeed," answered Michael to him. "But most of the battles between the good and the evil were lost. And that means the evil's army grows bigger and bigger with every war."

"So Voron's army is bigger than our Lord's army."

"Yes, indeed," said Michael. "But it is not so strong. And all of you saw that."

Many of those who were sitting there and heard the conversation approved what the angel had said, as it was true. Everyone saw the power of the angels.

Somewhere in Amnus, two young ones were staying in front of Efreu. The hamaan, with the power gave to him by The Highfather, was the wiseman that had the right to unite the two souls into only one . . .

"These two bodies will become only one soul. These two persons become only one family. These two will be ONE forever," said Efreu while he put some kind of crowns on the two young ones' heads.

"Take care of your woman," he said to Emos. "Listen your man," said Efreu to Adela.

The two people looked at each other, smiled, and then they began to embrace everyone who was there to congratulete them.

But this moment of happiness had to be a short one; even if such a happy moment required a party, the banits couldn't do that because of those who left this world; many of them had died.

"And with this beeing said, everyone should go with his family. Emos, now you also have a family. So go with them."

And everyone went to see their family.

"You are hurt," said Adela to his lover, Emos, while they were staying near the fire.

"Don't worry. Everything will be fine. These are not serious wounds. I'm not seriously injured."

"But your skin is burned, even on your face," said Adela. "I want to kiss you, but I'm afraid that I'll harm you touching your face."

Besides his scar on his face when he was young boy, a scar that began from his forehead above his right eye and came down over the eyelid and a little down over his cheek, now he had some burns on his face. The burns were not so obvios, but they were painful. But those burns and the scar didn't make him ugly. He's the same handsome boy; the scar showed everyone that the boy was a great warrior. For someone to have such a scar, surely he fought with a horrible creature. Because he was still alive, it meant that the creature was dead.

"Everything will be fine," Emos said to her. Then he embraced her with passion, kissing her on the cheek. "Everything will be fine," he repeated. "You can kiss me if you want. You can kiss your husband."

He smiled. And he kissed her with tenderness.

The last two or three days were without any attack. So everyone was staying with his or her familly because for many days they couldn't even see their relatives or their parents.

So Emos was with his wife. Her mother was with them. Cafgar, Adela's father, was also there. They can't be happy, but they are relieved because the nightmare was over. Those weeks were a real nightmare for everyone who decided to fight beside the Lord of Light.

"Emos, my son, thank you for taking care of my familly . . . your familly . . . because even if I didn't know this from the beginning, your are my son. And I'm more than glad that my daughter chose you."

These words meant a lot for Emos. He never could have been so happier. He had an intelligent, beautiful, and kind lover; the best mother anyone could ever want; and now this man called him his son. This was very important for him. The best thing that could ever happen to him.

Everyone was now happy, though they couldn't show it. They had to stay calm for a period as a sign of respect to those who lost their lives fighting this war.

Many of the banits, marnasits, and hamaans rested their body—almost all of them. As usual, the innocent children ran and played with their friends in the courtyard. The women prepared food for their families.

Michael and Gabriel smiled at the children. While they were playing their games, the children ran around the huge angels. And even if the angels were sitting down, they were still huge. Some of the children hid themselves behind their huge wings, others behind Gabriel's great shield. And the angels let the children play around them. You can actually say that they were playing with the children because when a child hid himself behind Michael's left wing, the angel approached his wing by his body so none of the others could reach him. After few seconds, Michael released the boy, who was more than happy because no one could catch him, and the boy ran away toward Gabriel. And lots of boy and girls ran after him to catch him, making lots of noise.

"Be like these children, and the kingdom of heaven will be yours," said Michael.

Some adults heard his words, but they didn't give much attention to them. They looked at the noisy and happy children; some of them smiled a little, and then everyone continued to do what they did before: cutting wood for fire, cooking—all kinds of stuffs.

It was so much quiet, so peaceful, and all the people were staying around fire camps.

The group of heroes—Efreu, Emos Billy, Rahnab, Shigash, Marnuk, and the others—were neighbors. Theirs tents were close. And if they didn't stay at the same fire at the beginning, now they were. They spoke about their fights, about what they saw in this journey, about everything. They even can say a joke or two.

After a while, Rahnab asked the others, "Why didn't Hingus come to stay with us."

And this was a good question. Hingus was staying alone near a little fire. Handsome Hingus—now he was not as handsome like two days ago. His face was burned now, worse than the others. From those who were touched by Voron's son, Hingus was seriously injured by the fire. You can't say he was ugly because of the burned skin and hair, but he was not the Hingus they all knew before.

"He is so quiet, and it looks he doesn't like our presence," said Rahnab.

"Hingus likes to be alone right now. He needs some days to get himself in shape. And we will give him that time," said Emos to Rahnab.

And they continued to discuss between them.

Hingus was alone near his fire. Once, few weeks ago, he never was alone. The girls were around him, waiting to be asked to be his wife. His father was one of the richest men in Megros. But now he was dead, and the fortune of Hingus family was buried by the death army in Megros castle.

Emos, his best friend, was there to stay with him, but Hingus asked him to leave. Even Billy asked him to come to eat with him, but it was useless. Adela brought him something to eat and some water, but the young didn't touch any of it. He was not hungry, he was not thirsty, he was—

"Why did all these happen to me? Why did the Lord let my father die? Why did he let Megros be destroyed? Everyone said he is the strongest, stronger than Voron. Why didn't he send these two angels to protect Megros? What kind of protector is he? It looks like Voron is more caring with his servents. He is more—"

But something stopped him.

"Poor Hingus . . . What happened with you? Look at you. You are no more beautiful," said a calm voice.

Hingus was angry. Who can make these jokes about him? He was injured. Who can make jokes about someone who was hurt?

Hingus took his spear. He was ready to—

"And your father is dead. Your mother—he died at your birth. You could never see her. And now you are dead, too. You are dead to everyone."

"Who are you? Show yourself!"

"Hingus, calm down. I'm here to help you," said the same calm voice.

"How can you help me? And how can you speak about my parents in such ways? What do you know about them?"

A person appeared in front of Hingus. When he saw that person, Hingus prepared his spear to teach that man a lesson, but he couldn't raise his hand against him. Something didn't let him hurt that person.

"I love your anger. It makes me feel powerful," said the person.

"Who are you?" asked Hingus.

"I'm someone that still loves you unlike your Lord, the one who lets your parents die so easily, the one that lets so many people die without any reason."

Hingus said nothing. He was still angry, but now he listened to the person. He was almost right. Why did his parents and so many friends have to die?

"Who are you?" he asked more calmly than at the beginning.

"I am Voron," said the person. And the person approaching was a woman, the most beautiful woman he had ever seen.

"You can't be Voron. Voron couldn't get inside Amnus because Amnus is our Lord's home on this planet. Evil couldn't enter inside this castle."

"Voron can be anywhere, even in temple of your Lord. Even in your 'temple.' Inside you . . . inside your heart. But let's speak about the reason I came to meet you."

"Yes, sure. And you want me to believe that you are Voron? Okay, fine, if you wish so," said the arrogant Hingus. "I'm listening."

"Look into my eyes, straight into my eyes, and see what I'm going to offer you."

Hingus looked straight into the woman's eyes, and what he saw was that he was handsome again. He was surronded by beautiful women. He was once again rich. He was the most important person from that town, a huge town, and everyone listened him. It was so—

But the dream stopped.

"All these things and more I am going to offer you in exchange of a small favor," said Voron. "I can also give you what you want the most. I can give you . . . Adela."

Hingus said nothing. He can't betray his friends, his Lord; but he wanted to have everything.

"Don't worry. I'm not going to ask you to betray any of your friends. I'm going to ask you a small thing. Just put some more woods on this fire and draw a circle with a stick on it."

Hingus looked at the woman. It was just that—put some more woods into that fire. He wanted to do that just before this woman, the one that pretended to be Voron, came. To put some more woods on the fire and a small circle—what harm could that do to anyone?

"I won't forget that. Thank you, my child."

Then she kissed him and disappeared.

Hingus put some more woods on the fire; then he grabbed a stick and drew a circle into the fire, in the ashes from the burned woods. And that's it.

"Run! Run, you fools! You have no power against him!" yelled Michael.

"All the hamaans, go and protect the women and children! You can't harm him! It's usless to try to fight against him! So leave! Now!" yelled Gabriel.

Everyone listened to the angels. But some of them did what the angels had said a little too late, and because of that, they died.

S'Hamoack was still alive. Someone resurrected him. And everywhere there was fire again. Many tents burned in few seconds, and some of them were burned inside; women, children, and old people were burned alive.

"Why did this happen? Why, my Lord, why?" yelled some of the women.

"Lord, please help us! Spare the life of our children. Please!" yelled the others.

Lots of the people were crying. Everywhere there was chaos. Flames, shouts, and tears, fear, and terror—why did these all happen again?

. . . .

"He is searching for something . . . or for someone! Chase him! I will help these people to extinguish the fire," said Michael to Gabriel.

Like the wind, Gabriel began to chase the fire creature. S'Hamoack sensed that he was being chased, so he ran faster and faster. Actually he moved faster and faster because the creature didn't run. He appeared in a place, then he disappeared from that place, and then he apeared in another place. This was his way of moving.

Gabriel chased the creature for few minutes. Then both of them stopped.

"I will end with you forever!" said Gabriel to the creature. And he attacked S'Hamoack.

The creature rejected the attack easily.

"He is more powerful," said Gabriel to himself. "What happened to him?"

He tried to attack the creature again, but it seemed that his swords didn't harm the creature.

Micahel came to help Gabriel against the creature, but he also was very surprised when he saw that Gabriel didn't smash the fire creature.

"He is stronger . . . much too stronger," said Gabriel to Michael.

They started to attack the creature like they did before, but it was usless. The creature succeeded in rejecting every attack.

S'Hamoack was stronger than ever. It looks like Voron made him much stronger that now he can fight against the Lord's captains easier than the first time.

Emos, Efreu, Shigash, Billy, and Marnuk arrived at the place where the creature was fighting against the two angels. Hingus was there too . . . All of them could see that the creature didn't run anymore. He could face the two angels, Michael and Gabriel.

One of the creature's arms became a fire shield, made by that strong magma. So when the angels tried to hit the creature with their weapon, S'Hamoack used his arm to reject the attack. And even if his shield was part of his body, this time the creature didn't yell because of the pain.

His other hand was a great mace, and the hit of this mace was so powerful that when he hit Gabriel's shield, it almost threw the angel to the ground.

"You have no power against me. My father made me stronger then you," said the creature. You can see now his entire face because now it doesn't run like the first time, and now you could hear an evil laugh coming from him.

"The faith in our Lord will help us destroy you—again!" said Gabriel to the fire creature.

"Is that so?" yelled the creature.

And after another evil laugh, the creature transformed his mace arm into a spear arm. And he hit Gabriel's shield so powerfully that the shield broke into pieces, and the spear went through Gabriel's chest, and Gabriel was hurt.

Because of the power of the angel, the spear broke, so a part of the creature's body was missing now. The angel hurt him, and the creature yelled because of the pain.

But for his enemies the loss was bigger. Gabriel fell down but only on his knees, beacuse of the huge rock spear from his body. He also was leaning on his sword. He was badly injured. He could hardly raise his eyes to look for the last time at Michael.

Michael, angered than ever, attacked S'Hmoack with his scepter so hard that the shield arm of the creature also became pieces. After that, the creature disappeared again.

Michael looked for the creature, but he didn't se it, so he went to Gabriel. Gabriel smiled to him and said, "If this was pur Lord's will, I will accept it."

And he died.

Then a great light came to take his body. His body rose and became lighter. After few moments, it disappeared forever.

"My Lord, give me the strength to kill Voron's son."

Then he looked once again for S'Hamoack. He saw him. He was in front of the group of heroes. So it seemed that even if the creature could easily kill Michael too, it chose to go near the heroes' group.

The angel ran after him. He wanted to kill the creature who killed his brother. Even if we know that the angels were created by God, the Lord of Light, to protect the others, this angel wanted to kill—to kill S'Hamoack.

"So you will be Voron's next son," said S'Hamoack, looking at the scared group of people.

And he instantly killed Emos. Adela saw what happened in front of her eyes. He saw that the creature kill her lover, her husband. Her mother and some other women grabbed her because the women wanted to go and help her men. And this would be a useless choice for her.

But everyone knows that when you love someone you don't think. You act. So surely everyone understood her choice. But the women stopped her.

"My father's will is done," said the fire creature. Then his body became some kind of fire wall. It surrounded Emos, and both S'Hamoack and Emos disappeared.

He apeared outside the Amnus walls where Voron's army waited for him, but when he wanted to to straight to his captain, which awaited for him, Hingus came in a hurry at the Amnus gate. Something or someone showed him where to go. When he reached the place, he attacked the fire creature with his spear.

But S'Hamoack killed him so easily.

"My Lord, we should do something to stop this bloodshed," said Michael to someone.

But there was nobody, or at least I can not see Him or hearing him.

I hear no answer, but I'm sure that Michael spoke with someone, someone who was his leader. Probably He was the Lord of Light, the Creator.

"Once again Voron doesn't care about the laws. The battle must be won by the people of this planet. But Voron sent his son to fight on his evil side. And because of that, our brother, your disciple died. Gabriel is not anymore with us."

There were few moments of silence, but I'm sure that Michael heard something.

"If this is Your will, then we shall do so," said the angel. "But I need to speak with my brothers, and this needs time."

But someone stopped him. Another few moments of quiet. After that Michael said, "So Kalus is also on Mania! Oh, my Lord, You know everything. You knew that Voron once again wouldn't obey Your Laws, so You kept some of Your angels on this planet. Kalus and my brothers are here."

Kalus was that creature from the ice cave, the creature that gave to Rahnab the last key of the Amnus gate, and it looked like that his true form was that of an angel.

"Where is my son?" asked Voron to one of his generals.

"I'm here, Father," answered S'Hamoack with his strong voice.

"Not you. My other son!" said Voron.

"There he is," answered the general called Uz'Khal. The hamaans told the others a story about him. They said that this creature was Voron's first creation. Voron put in him such power that any living creature staying next to him will die in few seconds. Even the hamaans, people chosen by the Lord to be his armies in these wars, were affected by Uz'Khal, the death. They didn't die like other living creatures by only staying next to him, but some storyes said that even some hamaans had died when they fought against him.

"Take him, general."

"What about the other—" asked the general, showing Hingus's body.

"His soul is mine, his body same. Take him too, and let's go because the Lord's army will be here soon. S'Hamoack, you wait here. You'll be the general of these armies. You'll fight untill all of you become pieces."

"We can stay and fight against them, too," said another general. Mhalath, the disease, was another general in Voron's army. Like the stories told by the hamaans to the others, everyone knew that

Mhalath also had a great power. The difference between Uz'Khal and Mhalath was that a living creature staying near Mhalath didn't die, at least not so quickly. Sombody who fought with Mhalath and is still alive, that person killes anyone who stays next to him . . . in few months. Hundreds or thousands, even ten thousand people, could die because of only one man that met Mhalath. His power was all kinds of unknown diseases and plagues.

"We have no power against that army. It is too strong for us . . . for now," said Voron.

And he disappeared. His generals and his guards, like those that had fought against Gabriel and Michael, did the same.

A final battle took place outside the Amnus walls. But this time the hamaans, the banits, and the marnasits only looked at the battle. Armies of angels sent by the Lord of Light were smashing Voron's army. S'Hamoack was also killed by five angels. One of them was Michael.

The hidrass's heads were cut one by other. The skeletons were made into pieces. Every weapon of those angels also smashed at least ten of those skeletons with only one hit.

What remained from the Army of Death, Voron's army, was now easily smashed by not more than a hundred angels.

"My Lord," said one of the generals, „the angels are coming after you."

"Yes, I know," said Voron.

"What should we do?" asked the same general.

"You may leave and take these bodies with you," said Voron.

And all the generals disappeared.

Voron was now alone in his throne's chamber from this planet. He was waiting for his angels. Every time a fight took place on one planet, the Lord of Light sent his angels to chain the evil for another thousands of years.

Suddenly the door of the chamber opened. Actually, it broke into pieces. And ten angels, all of them in shining armor, entered inside the room with Michael.

"I've been waiting for you," said Voron. He was smiling.

"Put him in chains," said Michael to the angels. Four of them approached Voron. Even if the angels were bigger than Voron, they were afraid because Voron took the form of the same women who had spoken with Hingus.

"Don't be afraid. We are stronger than him," said Michael to the angels.

"Gabriel was the first one. Now you're next, said Voron to those who put him the chains. He looked dismissive and haughty at them. He was stronger than any of the angels. Once he was one of them, but now he is on the other side. Everyone knows that God, the Lord of Light, punished him and chased him away from his kingdom. And now Voron was on the side created by himself: the evil side. Choosing this way, creating this way, he became stronger than any angel. He proved that using his son he was stronger even than Michael. At least he was stronger than Gabriel by killing him . . .

But so many angels were too much even for him.

Voron looked at Michael.

"I'm stronger than ever," said Voron to Michael. "And there is nothing you can do about it."

Michael said nothing. Perhaps his heart felt that Voron was stronger than ever. Or perhaps the Lord made Michael stronger than ever too because there must be someone to face Voron's strength.

"It's time to put you in your prison," said Michael to Voron.

"It's the first time that I'm so happy to be in your Lord's prison because after these one thousand years, once again we'll fight against you for my favorite planet. And you know the name of it."

"Yes, I know. It's the planet named Earth."

Voron smiled. Michael grabbed him by his arm and disappeared with him. The angels did the same.